I0701294

AN ELEPHANT. A ROCK. A MOUNTAIN.
A MISSILE. A REUNION.

EVERYDAY RAINBOWS

THOMAS J. GEBHARDT III

EVERYDAY RAINBOWS

Copyright © 2023 by Thomas J. Gebhardt III

The following collection and each story included therein is a work of fiction. All characters depicted as well as names, places and events mentioned are created from the author's imagination for story purposes. Any resemblance to persons living or dead, or to places or events past or present, is entirely coincidental.

This 1st edition has been catalogued with the Library of Congress.

Library of Congress Control Number: 2022919154

ISBN:

979-8-9857160-2-3 E-Book

979-8-9857160-3-0 Paperback

Publisher Ghoti

Honolulu, Hawaii, United States of America

All rights reserved. No part of this publication is permitted to be used, reproduced, scanned or transmitted in any form, digital or printed, or by any means without prior legal written consent from the author except in the case of brief quotations in critical articles and reviews.

Cover design by Damonza

Logo design by M. Takajiro Tobita

www.tjgiii.com

CONTENTS

Dedicated to Daniel Uyeunten

You wanted to help
You waited to help
With my top secret project

Here it is

TATE THE ELEPHANT

1

Republic of Mozambique
1974

IN THE BUSHES, between carefully placed branches and leaves was the barrel of a gun, and from it a rush of flame and metal. Loud shots echoed from hunters hidden in camouflage amongst yellow and green grass, behind red mounds, and atop gray-brown trees. The family of four galloped along the shallow pond, the mother leading the pack further out into the open, right into their trap. A jeep roared into view and skidded up a thick cloud of dust. Face to face with the beast of a machine, the adults bellowed and the little ones wailed. Another jeep appeared, herding them in the opposite direction—the jeeps and the creatures like a stampede, like war.

Bang. Bang, bang. A dart clung to his brother. A group of men held up wide nets that they wound back and hurled over his father. Both disappeared as he struggled to keep up with his mother that curved left. One of the jeeps pulled around in front then cut them off. His mother narrowly dodged as a dart bounced off of the hood, then slipped into the haze of swirling dirt. Unable to control his trajectory, he collided into the side door and staggered backwards. His ears flapped down, his tail flopped. He fell to his knees, trembled as barrels pointed at him and laughed, as engines revved and revved. Then, a final dart.

Yellow feathers clung to his skin as he wobbled side to side. His vision blurred, he felt wooziness coming on, taking over like sweet nectar. He rolled over onto his side, his breathing steady. His lids closed but he remained awake, could still hear.

"There we are. Got the bugger . . ." A boot crunched pebbles near his head. "Easy, little fella. Down you go. Easy."

"What of the others?"

"Ah, we don't want 'em. Just the runts."

A new voice, more crunching. "Looks like the sibling didn't make it. Too many tranqs. Stopped breathing."

"Blast. Bugger off . . ."

"Guessin' our payday be a bit on the slim side, eh."

"Well, it'll have to do. He'll make up for two."

Words turned to mere sounds then faded off and away. Consciousness began to float above and behind, through it all, permeating. His heartbeat slowed until it was almost a murmur. His lungs rose, fell, filled, swelled. And then nothing . . . nothing at all.

He awoke in darkness, on his side, on a thin layer of hay, confined in some small wooden crate. He hit his head, unable to wriggle or squirm. Something was off, a feeling unfamiliar to him. Not just solitude but disorientation. The ground seemed to rock back and forth in a nauseating slosh of motion, gravity seemed to be cradling him in jerky bumps. He felt a rumble in his stomach then the muscles in his abdomen contort. The inside of his throat constricted, then uncontrollably he vomited. Warm bile splashed out and spilt under him, and he lay there in the mix of liquid and dissolving solids.

With loud banging and creaking, the side of the crate burst open and fell, to several men with sticks, with nets, with guns awaiting. He shivered and whimpered as he hobbled to his feet, down a ramp, and into a cage with other elephant calves. It was so hot and there was no water. He was so hungry but there was no food. The metal clanged as the gate slammed shut. The men banged on the corner posts, and rattled and shook the walls. The calves backed together in the middle, helpless.

"Ha, that's right, Dumbos. Li'l money-bags."

2

Hemingway, FL
1992

THE GLOCK TREMBLED in his small hands, between his legs.
He felt the grip of the handle, saw the gleam on the barrel, felt
the weight of it. A faint reflection stared back at him, as the
neighborhood slums glided by in the night. He licked his lips,
took a long hard swallow, felt the vehicle slow then come to a
halt. There was silence as the car idled, as he pulled down the
brim of his beanie, tucked the gun into the back of his jeans.

"Ya got this, T? Y'know what to do?"

"Yeah, dawg." His voice was on the brink of cracking.

"Just go up in the motherfucker, get the fuckin' money in
the bag, then get the fuck up outta there . . . We'll be waitin'
on you."

"Yeah, baby. 'Bout to be a man, mang."

"Time to graduate, yo."

He placed a hand on the door handle, clicked it open,
took a breath, felt an encouraging hand clap him on the back.
Stepping out, he closed the door and slipped the hood of his
hoodie over his head. His hands rubbed together then slid into

his pockets as he stepped past the stop sign, off the curb, and across the street towards the convenience store. It was a dingy, dimly lit place with a small two-pump gas station out front.

There was a slight jingle when he pushed the door open and went inside. The old man behind the counter was going through receipts, adding on a small calculator that clacked. Some lady placed items in a basket: a banana, some gum, a lighter, a bottle of water. He stood near the magazines, flipped through them, waited for the lady to go and pay. Eyes on the back of his head tracked her movement, from behind the aisle by the refrigerator towards the front—a cold sweat, an increase in his breathing and heart rate.

With the light ding from the register drawer, he turned and pulled out his weapon. He shouted with a slight slur, some spittle flying from his lips as he aimed. He nudged the lady in the back, told her to put her hands up, yelled at the man. The lady shrieked, did as she was told. The man, though, glared down at him with a calmness, as if staring at a rodent pest. He slammed the register back closed.

"'Ey, what the hell you doin', old man!" The weapon trembled in his hand. "Gimme the motherfuckin' money!!!"

The man then reached behind the counter, pressed a button and pulled out a snub-nosed revolver, pointed it back at the kid. A ringing echoed outside the store and through the gas station. The lady closed her eyes now, begging, *Oh God, please, please don't kill me.* The old man and the kid pointed still.

"Hurry up!" The trembling grew more pronounced, the man's glare more confident. "C'mon, the money!"

A trickle of sweat dripped down the side of his face, and with that his finger twitched and pulled the trigger. Behind the old man, a shelf collapsed and groceries fell to the floor. As the lady screamed, he nudged her and ran out the door, to another slight jingle. Across the street, the car pulled away with a loud screech in the other direction, a hub cap rolling off.

The ringing was louder outside, and behind him, he heard the jingle from the door. There was a shot then another, the cracking of asphalt, and then he ran down the street. Angry foreign yelling chased after him as the soles of his feet slapped the pavement. In the distance, he could hear sirens blaring now.

His breath grew heavy as his running turned into a sprint. He hopped over a small wall then climbed a fence. There were laundry lines with clothes hanging up that he pushed through, snapping some of the pins and knocking articles to the dirt. There was another siren. It felt like they were circling, search-ing for him like predatory birds in the sky. He knelt down with his hands on his thighs, panting now, feeling a burning inside his chest, heart about to burst. Leaning his head back, he strafed the side of the small house and peaked around the corner. A patrol car rolled by shining a flashlight. The glow grazed the sleeve of his hoodie, and then there was a voice on a megaphone.

He frantically bolted, hopped another small wall, hurdled the hood of a car setting off the alarm. Some motion sensor lights in a garage popped up and zeroed him out. They were right on his tail so he sprinted even faster. He jumped into the street, dodged oncoming headlights, then disappeared into a playground, towards the park behind it. He felt safer now in the darkness with the cover of trees, checked backward but no one was there. His running slowed to a jog then a hurried walk. A shooting pain ran up the side of his ribs, and there was a cramp in his calf muscle. He limped towards a wall in the back.

There was a pipe that protruded from the ground in an upside down U-shape. He stepped on this then hoisted himself up, balanced on the horizontal pole at the top of the fence, straddled it, slipped over, then landed on the grass below. As he stooped and dusted himself off, he glanced around and noticed all was different, like he had entered another world . . . His wide eyes panned the scene in one long sweep.

What was once a nightmare now was the most vivid and surreal dream. Panic, fear and dread dissipated, became wonder and astonishment. He had slipped into a portal, stepped into another realm.

Bright lights from booths with food and games. Tents pitched up. Clowns, animals, rides. There was music and balloons. Couples walking by, families with children in hand and babies in strollers. *What the hell???* He tucked the weapon away in the back of his jeans again, slid his hoodie over it, tried to blend in. *What is this place?* The community center, perhaps. He walked with his head tilted one way then the other, in awe, mesmerized, by the sights and sounds occurring all around him like an arcade—like the inside of a pinball machine.

There was a miraculous sensation of splendor, but there was also eeriness. What brought him here? And for what purpose?

A breeze blew through and carried with it a shiny red balloon that bounced like a tumbleweed. It seemed to stand out from the surrounding background and drew him in, like it was beckoning. He wanted to touch it, to have it. His gaze would not break free.

It began to drift. Without blinking, he followed and tried to catch it, catch up to it. It continued to lure him . . . Further and further into the pinball machine he went, until he was no longer sure where he was. It was quiet now in this area, dark, with machines humming and cords tangled and strewn about. He touched the slippery balloon, but doing so fell through the side of one of the tents. Lying on the ground on straws of hay, he groaned. The balloon floated to the feet of a man that stood there staring, an eyebrow lifted.

Before him, the gun had slipped out and was exposed. He picked it up then got to his feet, pointed it with both hands.

"Why you do this, child?" The man's voice was comforting, peaceful. "You put that down. Come on now."

His brow wrinkled as his lips curled into a snarl. He squeezed the handle of the gun harder, touched his finger to the trigger, aimed it carefully as he gritted his teeth.

"No, child, this is not the way . . . Come now."

The man held out his hand, smiled, motioned with an open palm despite the weapon drawn, now shaking. He wanted to shoot the man—wanted his brains on the floor in a pile of mush—but somehow he couldn't. He inched closer, lowered the weapon, closed his eyes, then felt his shoulders begin to shudder. A tear dripped off his cheek and soaked into the dirt, where the gun plopped down a second later with a dull thud. His knees buckled and he collapsed onto the dirt, whimpered there on all fours like a frightened animal.

Before he knew, the man joined him and held him close as he continued to cry moist muffled sobs into his belly. The man wrapped an arm around his shoulders, put a hand on the back of his tiny head, glanced sideways at the gun, then closed his own eyes.

"It's okay, child . . . You're okay . . ." The man rocked him, patted him and rubbed his head. "Everything's going to be okay."

3

Morocco was his name, and he had a shaved head with gold earrings and tattoos. He was tall with broad shoulders, had muscular arms and a general bulky build. Physically, he was rather threatening due to his size and features, but his demeanor and aura were that of patience and kindness. He was what they called a gentle giant. Morocco turned from the kerosene stove, faced down to the boy who was still wiping tears from his cheeks, still quiet. He continued to stir the contents of the pan then poured it onto two plates, stuck it with spoons. When he sat down near the boy at the small table on the floor and offered a plate, the boy didn't respond. He just lay it in front of him.

"Well, I told you *my* name. What's yours?"

No response, just blank staring. There was a blink, then his eyes shifted downward and gazed at his hands on his lap.

He left the boy alone, pressed no further, instead began to eat. He scooped a bit of it and blew, inadvertently sending some steam and aroma in front of the boy, then took his time chewing and swallowing. He, too, stared on ahead, the two of them sitting there in mutual silence.

Who was this kid? And why did he, *how* did he, appear at random all of a sudden?

"T-Timothy . . ." the boy blurted out. "I'm Tim."

"Oh, Timmy. What a nice—"

"No, not *Timmy*. Timothy. Or just Tim." Morocco held back a smile at the boy's annoyance of this. "I hate that. My mama calls me that."

"Sorry, child, I apologize. Timothy it is." He watched as the boy took a spoonful in his hand. "And how old are you?"

"Ten. And a half."

"Ah, what a grand age. I remember such a time." Morocco smiled, nodded. "And how is it? I know it's not what you would call gourmet . . ."

"S'okay, thanks." He chewed, swallowed. "Look, mister, I'm sorry—"

"No need to be sorry, child." Morocco pushed the plate away, tapped on his belly like a big drum. "Ever been to the circus, Timothy?"

"Not never." His mouth was half-full as he spoke. "My very first time."

"Oh, yeah? Well, you're in for a treat. I'm one of the handlers and trainers here. Been doin' this most my life. Wanna meet some a the animals?"

The boy faced up, spoon still in his mouth. ". . . Uh, yeah. That'd be kinda cool."

Morocco handed him the red balloon, which dangled in mid-air bouncing off the ground tethered by a dinky string. On their short walk, the boy saw acrobats practicing atop the trapeze, others walking with long balance poles over a tight-rope, a shirtless man blowing balls of fire from a torch, and a couple clowns juggling on unicycles. There was a large multicolored tent on the far side, and it was full of cages with different animals inside: lions, horses, birds. He watched a lion lay on its side on its makeshift throne. The birds formed a unique chorus with their flapping and chirping. He went up close to the horses, held out his hand, pet one on their snout.

"Like animals, Timothy?"

"I guess so . . ." He pet its neck and back, stared at the horse's face real close. "We had a dog before. I'm allergic to cats. We had fish, birds." He faced down to the ground, his hand still touching the animal. "Then when my daddy left, my moms couldn't afford to keep our dog no more. Had to let 'im go."

"That's too bad. Just . . . you and your mother, then?"

"Yep. Just me and my bitch-ass moms."

"Child, you mustn't refer to your mother this way."

"Easy for you to say. *You* try living with her."

Morocco stepped closer, also pet the horse. "I had a mother once, and she was the sweetest thing. I loved my mother."

The boy dazed up at him, an eyebrow raised, then returned to the animal. The two of them stood there, quiet, petting along its neck, stroking.

"So, you take care of all these?"

"Well, I help sometimes. I'm actually in charge of the elephants."

"Elephants???"

Morocco just smiled in response.

When Morocco smiled, it was as if he was pleased with all things, himself, his surroundings, and the entire world as he knew. He had thick lips that stretched round cheeks, and he had big teeth, one of which was silver. Drawing the curtain to one side, he bowed and let Tim pass through to the darkened tent. Tim walked in, carefully stepped with the balls of his feet, feeling the dirt. Behind him, Morocco pulled a lever which sent a surge of power into the electrical cables and flashed the room alive.

A symphony of loud roars blared like strident brass notes from trumpets and trombones. Tim moved forward, mouth agape, hands dropped at his sides, as he stared at the quartet of magnificent beasts: two of them flailing their trunks, another hiding in the back, one of them on its hind legs for a brief moment. *Wow . . . Holy!* He peered into their eyes, big, black and round. He watched their floppy ears dangle and flap from the sides of their gigantic heads. Then, he took a timid step closer.

Morocco stepped past, unlocked the gate in front of the cage and went inside. He touched the creatures on their foreheads and stood beneath them, hugging at their underbellies. He did so with a loud, deep laugh and that same big ol' smile, then motioned for Tim to join.

Tim shook his head, stood there like a stolid crane, but after a moment walked over step by step. He put a hand on the gate, heard the squeaky grind of the metal hinge. It was like he was a dwarf in the land of giants. Holding a hand up, he breathed quick gasps in sharp hisses. From the side, a trunk snatched the beanie off his head, then another slipped in his hoodie and felt around his back. He squirmed as this happened, as if there was a snake or some worm that slithered on his skin, began to giggle.

"Hey, guy! That tickles!"

From behind the troupe, the elephant that had been hiding stepped forth. Its trunk hovered over and touched him on the shoulder, then slid towards his other shoulder and down his arm.

"Well, look at that . . . He likes you. Hmm."

Morocco leaned back on the metal bars, arms crossed, continued to smile. He watched as Tim laughed and played with one elephant then the other, but most of all the shier one that had been hiding. He hugged their limbs, pet their trunks, rubbed their bellies and their sides, laid down near them until he exhausted himself.

4

His body awoke with a stir, surroundings unfamiliar as his eyes darted around the room. There, on a seat with his back turned, was Morocco. He sipped from steaming hot coffee in one hand and stared into a newspaper in the other. Tim rolled, threw the covers to one side, sat with his hands flat on the bed, head down. He then glanced back up, yawned an unruly yawn, and rubbed at his eyes.

"Ah. Good morning, child." Morocco put down the mug and turned the pages, loud rustling and crinkling.

"W-what happened . . . ?"

"You fell asleep, playing with Tate."

"Tate?"

"Yes, one of the elephants. You don't remember?"

"Oh . . ." A smile crept over his face. He walked over, sat on a chair opposite.

"Did you sleep all right?"

Tim could just see half a face obscured by headlines. "Yeah, I guess so."

"Well, then," Morocco said, laying the paper down, "I do suppose that the time has come."

Tim watched as he stood, walked across the room, reached into a dresser, and returned. In his hands was the Glock 17. He studied it for a while, then held it at the barrel with the handle out, offering it over. Tim stared at it, then reached and took it.

"You be safe now. Take care, child."

"Morocco . . ."

"Yes?" He had returned to his paper.

"Do you think . . . I could stay here with you? I mean, a little longer."

The man leaned back in his chair, a *hrmm* sound leaking out of his lips, pursed at the question. He folded the paper, pushed it aside, then interlocked his fingers, resting the bridge of his nose on his knuckles. Pondering for a moment, he stared past the kid to the far side of the room.

"I'm not sure this is wise." He folded his arms, shook his head. "You should return home, to your mother."

"Please." Tim gulped. "Please, please."

"The circus is no place—"

"Please! I've got nothing else! This . . ." He wiped at one of his cheeks with a balled up fist. "This is the first time, in a really long time . . . I felt calm, happy. Maybe ever."

Morocco gazed across at Tim, who stood now with hands together in a pleading motion, but shook his head again.

"Child, what of your schooling—?"

"It's summer vacation."

He rubbed the jawline of his chin with his fingers then his palm, making a clicking sound with his tongue. Then, he leaned forward and breathed out a long sigh.

"All right, all right . . . Fine, child. But on one condition."

"Yes. What? Anything."

"You must call your mother. Tell her where you are and what you are doing." He stood, put a pan on the stove. "If she says it is okay, then okay."

Tim smiled at this.

"A few days. Couple weeks, most."

5

Tim had become an unofficial apprentice to Morocco and assisted with handling and caring for the elephants. He dragged over a hose that he struggled to aim, spilling more than what was leftover in the water troughs. He peeled bananas and fruit for the creatures and spread plenty of hay. Afterward, it always fascinated him how they used their trunk for so many things. Eating, drinking, washing themselves. Like a big tentacle suction cup.

"Timothy." The boy didn't respond right away, mesmerized by the tentacle motion. "Timothy. Come, child."

With a light jerky movement, he glanced over then joined Morocco who was holding a bullhook—something like a hook attached to a handle with a tapered end. He gazed at this, curious, then faced away.

"Sir, yes, sir!" Tim said, hand in salute. "Reporting for duty, sir!"

Morocco shook his head with a small smile. "Okay, today you help me train the animals. Think you're ready?"

"Yup. Hell yeah I'm ready."

He proceeded to show the boy basic commands and tell him general rules: tap the ear, tap the shoulder, wave this way, that way, say this, that with a low, loud voice, and always remain stern yet calm. Tim mimicked as best he could, like a very intense game of Simon Says.

After a good half an hour or so, they rested under a tree, the lesson continuing in lecture form. Both stared out over the grassy field, side by side, enjoying the cover of shade and the slightest breeze.

"Remember. These aren't beasts but intelligent creatures. They have feelings. They remember, they learn."

Tim shifted over then faced forward again. He pulled out a wad of grass and tossed it back onto the patchy ground.

"Most importantly, Timmy . . . er, Timothy . . . is to give 'em lots of love. Because the truth, they're meant to be out in the open. Imagine all this . . ." He motioned with a nod of the chin, licked his lips. "But a hundred, a thousand times greater."

His eyes widened. "Whooa . . ."

"Mm-hmm." Morocco's voice resonated. "Other trainers believe in hard, using fear and intimidation to control. But I focus on relationship, on trust."

He turned. "Like what do they do?"

"Beat them. Deprive them of food, water. I've seen creatures crouched down, weeping, terrorized from the abuse." Morocco shook his head, tightened his lips. "It's wrong, Timothy. So, so wrong."

The boy leaned forward, arms on his knees.

"This whole thing is wrong. They're not meant to be caged most the day. They're not meant to be in such small cages, or *any* cage."

". . . Is that what happened to Tate? Why you don't use him?"

"Yes, sad to say. He endured some of the cruelest trainers I've known, subjected to the worst kind of treatment."

Tim balled his fists, bit down on his lower lip, glared.

"Finally, one day, he snapped. Attacked his trainer, stormed out of the show. Me and another followed. I was able to calm him down, but it just never was the same after that. Management insists I include him, but I absolutely will not. I refuse."

A silence befell them. The wind had stopped.

"To them, it's a mere matter of money . . . But what of the safety of the people? What of the well-being of the animal?" He shook his head again, stared, leaned back. "Listen, child. Listen close. You must beware the greed of the white man. Beware the greed of all people."

Morocco could see the boy's eyes glisten as he told him this.

"Beware their greed. Beware their wrath, child."

6

MISTY SPRAY FORMED an ethereal rainbow that disappeared as each droplet floated downward. Tim aimed and shot a blast of water around the cage that rattled the metal and gushed. He continued to do so until most debris had been moved to one side, then he brought over a shovel and bin. Before he began, he wiped the sweat from his forehead and cheeks, leaned on the handle.

"Good work."

Tim turned back, saw Morocco standing there. "Oh, hey."

"Why don't you take a rest, child."

"Nah, I'm almost—"

"Oh, come now. Get some food in you." Morocco held an arm up, motioned with a wave. "Ah, there we are."

"What'd ya cook?"

"None of my bad cooking today. Let's go to the grounds instead."

"Really???"

"Why, yes. Time for a treat. You've earned it."

The two walked between bustling tents with booths set up. With chiming whimsical melodies filling the air, Tim stepped aside as carnies walked past. There was a group of kids about his own age tossing rings, a middle-aged man winding back and throwing a ball at stacked up bowling pins. Morocco pointed at a horse racing game then a row of large water guns aimed at round targets.

"Can I . . . ?"

"Sure, sure."

He unleashed a river into the mouth of the smiling clown target until the top of its head lit up and dinged. The worker handed over a small teddy bear. Morocco was in the next booth over and smashed a large mallet downward, causing similar lights and ringing.

They continued on toward a circle of food wagons and bought two slices of pizza, popcorn, a slushie, a corn dog and some cotton candy. Tim couldn't be happier and scarfed it all down in record time—like he hadn't eaten in weeks, months.

"What kinda tricks do elephants do?"

"All kinds, child. Many different ones." Morocco opened his eyes big, grinned. "Spectacular, amazing. It would blow your mind."

"Think you can show me?"

"Why, of course. You know, we should play with Tate. Maybe he'll show you one of his very special moves."

After watching the crowds pass by (it was particularly crowded that day) they returned to their tent. In the space behind, Tim waited, slurping the last of his icy blue drink. Morocco led the elephant out. Tim stood up, ran over and hugged Tate. A loud trumpeting followed joint laughter as the three formed a small circle.

He raised the baton, and the elephant lowered his head. Tim watched with his jaw dropped, then glanced at Morocco who smiled and nodded.

"Go on now. Don't be afraid."

Tim climbed up the side, but almost slipped and lost a shoe. Morocco hoisted him up onto the creature's back. The boy sat with a leg on either side, held around with arms spread and hands clutched. He had never ridden an animal before, let alone an elephant. *Woow!* His mouth agape, his tongue dancing behind white teeth, he squealed and chortled.

Tate hobbled in a small oval around Morocco, taking the boy for a short smooth ride, and then lunged up high on its hind legs. The boy shouted, squinting his eyes, squeezed tight.

"For this one, I've always had a soft spot. He's an African, you see. The others all Asian." Morocco walked over, rubbed its forehead. "So, we have that little something in common. I can feel it, I can see it."

Tim gazed down from atop his throne, listening with his head inclined to one side. The elephant moved its trunk about, shuffled in place.

"Neither of us belong. Both taken from our native home."

"Like . . . slavery?"

"Yes, Timothy. Like slavery. Only, for Tate, it's worse. Far, far worse." He rubbed at the ears now. "They're hunted for sport, for ivory. For these silly little shows."

Tim scanned around at each tent then off at the horizon, felt warm liquid drip. He sniffled then wiped his cheeks.

"I cry, too, child. I cry as our ancestors cry. You see the tears, you feel them. In each captured animal, in every stuffed trophy case, in all pieces of harvested meat . . . And, in every young man like yourself."

Morocco reached up, rubbed below Tim's eye. Tim faced down, swallowed a gulp of air.

"Tears of our ancestors, child. Tears of our ancestors."

7

Tim paced back and forth in front of the glass, then went inside and stared at the phone on the hook. He reached into his pocket, took out a quarter which he held at the coin slot but hesitated to drop in. Biting his lower lip, he listened as metal clinked, then heard the dial tone buzz on. As he pressed each button, he could hear dull beeps then muffled ringing. There was a voice, but he didn't respond. He refused to engage it. He merely listened as his eyes began to water, then he hung up.

It was getting dark, but the sun was still out. He felt at the back of his jeans, rubbed the handle of the gun. The ridged edges, the grip, the trigger—it filled him with exhilaration and dread. He breathed out a long sigh, rubbed his hands together as he paced back and forth again. His eyes followed his feet with each deliberate step, leaving a trail of sporadic prints in the red dirt. To one side, he noticed a snapped twig. Kneeling down, he took the twig in his hand, held it like a knife. The sharpened splintery end was jagged with a diagonal hollow. His fingers slipped around it tight, until his hand began to tremble. With a sudden quick jerk, he stabbed it into the dirt.

The end of the stick dragged across the surface. He stuck his tongue out in concentration, continued to stab and slice.

Then he stood and gazed down at it: a small stick figure next to a large rectangle with a squiggly line attached.

You and me, Tate.

Ain't no one gonna fuck with us no mo'.

8

When Tim awoke the next morning, Morocco was talking on the phone. His deep voice resonated in the small makeshift nook of the kitchen. He held the phone close to his ear with his back turned. His words were cut short, spewed in stuttered sentence fragments. Then he put the phone back on the hook, hung his head down low. Tim watched this from the other side of the room, sat up in his bed. Morocco raised his glass to take a sip, then threw it into the sink shattering it. As he walked out, Tim followed and tugged on the back of his pants.

"W-what happened? Wait!"

"Not now, Timothy."

"Tell me, 'Rocco!" His eyes narrowed. "Tell me, goddammit!"

"Language." The man faced down, touched the top of Tim's head, exhaled. "Okay. Okay, okay . . ."

Tim instinctively hugged him and began to cry.

"I'm afraid I have some bad news. That was the boss. They've decided to let me go." Morocco knelt down, held him close. "But it's okay. It's all going to be okay."

"What does that mean? W-what's gonna happen?"

"It means I have to leave. It means someone else will be taking over."

"But I don't want that! I don't want you to go, I don't want to have to go!!!" The petulant whine turned to a shout then a sad sob. "I don't want . . ."

"I know, child. I know. Neither do I."

⁂

Rocking on the floor, he wrapped his arms around his knees, his head down sideways. In front, he watched Tate and one of the others play with the water, splashing it on each other and on themselves. The movement of their trunks was mesmerizing, strange. The flat rounded bottoms of their feet hovering, stomping like a factory press. Their knees mechanically bent as they turned and walked, their tails wagging side to side. With the sky behind lit up bright orange, the stringy hairs on their backs and heads appeared like fiery dust.

Tate came up close, hobbled past his line of sight. Tim remained in his position like a crumpled paper ball, staring beyond, lost somewhere deep in thought, away, in a faraway place. He peered into each rustling crack on the creature's thick gray skin, then deep into its wet black eye that peered back into his own mind's eye. He watched its snout wrap around and bunch grass, bring it towards its mouth. As it chewed and swallowed, a ball of dust swept up and brushed against them, stinging Tim's eyes. He rubbed them, squinted, then glanced down.

"Beautiful, isn't it?"

Tim turned, noticed Morocco behind him.

"I could watch them all, all day long. Just . . . majestic."

"Yeah . . ."

"See. Animals, like these, I understand. Plants and rocks

and the ocean and sky. The earth. Mother Nature. It's people I don't understand, people I don't approve of."

Tim nodded, lifting his head up, remaining folded on the ground, distorted, like a gothic statue posing.

"'Rocco?"

"Yes, child."

"What's gonna happen to Tate?" His voice was soft.

"I wonder that, too." He placed a hand on the boy's head, then down on his shoulder. "The new trainer's coming in tomorrow. I will talk to him."

9

Morocco's usual wide grin was now a grimace, a flat frown. Across from him was the man that would take his place, a man named Lenny. Tim sat on the other side of the room, pretending to read a comic, but put it down and walked outside, still in earshot. Morocco hunched forward, one elbow on his knee. Lenny leaned in his chair with both arms up at his sides. Two cups sat on the table between them.

He studied the man: the long messy hair, the crooked disheveled mustache, the big pointy nose, every faded scar on his sunburnt skin.

"This coffee's shit."

Morocco said nothing, sipped.

"All righty, then. Let's get to it."

The two went around back, to the elephant encampment. Tim wandered off. Lenny walked in front, clanged his baton on the bars of each cage back and forth like an out-of-tune xylophone, stared each creature in the eye as if trying to hypnotize them.

"So, tent cage at night. Back lot during the day for a li'l training and some free time . . ." Lenny turned. "Hey. Where's your fourth?"

"Listen. About that—"

"Rules are clear. Gotta have four. Not three, four."

"I understand, but—"

"Ah, there. The hell he doing all the way over there? And the hell that punk kid doing???" Lenny turned, narrowed his eyes. "Ya let your son play wit' these fucking things?"

"I taught him myself. It's fine. As for that elephant, though, he needs—"

Lenny turned back, continued to walk forward. "Hey! Kid!"

Startled, Tim dropped what he was doing and an instantaneous cold sweat trickled down his face and palms.

"The hell ya doin'!?" The Southern drawl spewed. "Git outta there!"

"I-I . . ."

"Timothy, it's okay—"

"Like hell it's okay. It's *not* fucking okay. These things are dangerous, kid. Make no mistake about it, we're talking ten thousand pounds of mindless animal. Ya need to keep 'em in check. Ya need to keep 'em in line, keep 'em afraid . . . That or end up dead. You do *not* play with them, you hear me."

Morocco felt his chest collapse inward as Lenny held up the baton, brushed past Tim, and staggered towards Tate in anger.

"You! Back in line, now!" He pointed the stick causing Tate to back away, flapping his ears outward. "I said *now!*"

"Wait a minute. Hold on." Morocco grabbed Lenny by the arm, leaned in. "Wait. I said wait, damn it."

The man broke free with a quick jerk, glared.

"Listen. About this elephant . . . He has had it very rough, he is unfit to perform. You cannot use him. I'm warning you. Give him space, give him—"

"Aw, come on. Ya shittin' me? They all had it 'rough.' He ain't no different." Lenny turned back, raised the baton. "I know just how to deal with 'im."

"Tate . . ." Morocco grabbed Lenny by the arm again. "Tate is . . . special. It is a matter of safety here. I'm telling you, don't work with him. Do not come down on him. Seriously."

"Let go a me." Lenny pointed a stern finger, began to shake his head. "You are fucking crazy. No wonder ya got canned."

Tim shivered at Morocco's side, hid behind him.

"Get 'im back in the cage." Lenny bit down on his lower lip. "Yer done here."

10

THERE WAS A morose feeling lingering in the air, as Morocco placed the last few items in his suitcase, smashed it in then zipped up. Tim put on his hoodie, slipped on his beanie, watched with somber eyes. The man patted the boy on his shoulder, then led them out back where they both stood one last time with Tate in his cage, big metal bars between them. Reaching behind in his jeans, Tim touched the gun, restrained a glare. Morocco put one hand through the bars, rubbed at the forehead and trunk.

"Go on, child. Say your goodbyes."

"No . . . No." Tim bit his lower lip, faced away. "Hell no."

"Tate. Old friend. My good friend . . . I will miss you." Morocco turned to Tim, glanced as he kicked at the dirt. "You be a good boy, okay?"

With that, the two walked away through the grounds. It was early in the morning so there were no carnies, no booths or games lit up with chimey songs. There were no jugglers, there were no balloons or balloon animals. The sun just beyond the horizon burned away the crispness of dawn and the morning dew.

Around the entrance in front of booths with admission

tickets to go on sale, Morocco knelt down and faced the boy, placed an arm on each shoulder, then pulled him into a long hug. Tim closed his eyes, and after a moment's hesitation brought his arms up and hugged back—the two of them there, on the empty grounds, in the wee hour.

"Timothy. I want to tell you how thankful I am."

"Thankful? To me?"

"Yes. Yes. You see, I have a daughter . . . er, I had a daughter. She was around your age when I last saw her. She lives with her aunt and uncle now." Morocco licked his lips, blinked, took a deep breath. "It's so easy to forget just what it is you have, and to take those things for granted."

Tim just listened, said nothing.

"I maybe have spent too long, been too far away. But I think I'd like to go and see her now, make amends. What a fool I am and have been. All this time." Morocco faced away, unable to quite look the boy in the eye.

He wanted to ask what happened but chose not to, watched as tears dripped from the corners of the man's lids now closed, streaming down his round face. With a soft sniffle, he dragged a forearm across his cheeks, and Tim noticed for the first time that there was a plain gold ring on his finger. The boy's eyes widened, his lower lip hung open.

"So again, thank you . . . Thank you, Timothy . . . Thank you very, very much. For everything. For oh, so much."

Morocco smiled, but a fraction of his usual smile.

"And Timothy, also . . . I think it is time. You really must go home now."

The boy gazed down, felt his lip begin to quiver.

"A child needs his mother, as a mother needs her child." Morocco shook the boy's shoulders as he said this. "If there's anything you've learned here, it's this. We, every human being or creature on this earth, we all need love. There's no other way."

He nodded, felt his lips begin to curl, felt his eyes fill with warm fluid. The two embraced in a long hug once more, the sun now breaking through and shining over and onto them. A warmth like fresh steaming water from a springing geyser, if but for a moment. They swayed as they hugged, and when they broke, they both forced a smile.

"Here, child." Morocco took the boy's hand, placed in it a wad of money, then closed his fingers around it, placed his other hand on top. "Promise me."

Tim faced up, waited.

"Promise me you'll take care. Promise me you'll go home, and take care of your mother. Promise me that you've learned something from all this, from our time together. That this wasn't just a waste, that this wasn't all for nothing. Promise."

Tim's chest filled with a slow breath. His lips thinned, his eyes shifted to the dirt. Morocco felt a nagging ache at this delayed response, felt his forced smile fade.

"I promise."

11

WHEN TIM RETURNED to the entrance area, it was already late in the afternoon. His thumbs and fingertips felt sore from mashing rounds into each magazine. The gun weighed heavier with each nervous step towards the booth to buy a ticket for the big show. He made his way around, absorbed all the lights and color, listening to the songs, listening to the dinging and crashing and laughter and screams. This time, though, he wasn't filled with wonder or amazement but bitterness.

He waited in line, watched spitefully as children played back and forth and as couples held hands walking along care-free. He spent the last of the money on one more slushie, then sipped on the icy blue drink as he stepped towards the big striped tent. With the sun slipping away, the warmth pulled from him, leaving just the sloshy chill of condensation in his hand. As he entered, sat down on the bleachers facing the stage that was being set up, a spotlight shone on a single micro-phone stand.

Tim swilled his melting slushie, scanned around, noticed the bleachers filling up. The generic aluminum seemed flimsy for its height, rattled with each step. Multiple sets of these surrounded the stage in a wide open half-circle. The stage in middle had a single ramp leading up to it from what appeared to be a small building. The wooden ramp, the concrete walls, and the tent fabric appeared to contrast.

He played with the straw with his tongue and lips, leaned back, then relaxed his shoulders and slumped in his seat. Every thought seemed to seep up now that he was still: how things had gone wrong at the robbery, the chase, the circus, the shiny red balloon, Morocco's big round face and his cheeks and smile, Tate, the others, his mother that he should call, that he should go home to even now, and that bastard Lenny. All these bastards.

This is it, Tate. Your last show. I'm bustin' you outta here.

Staring again, lost in thought, away, in that faraway place, he rubbed at his forehead with his palm. Brain freeze collided in his skull like a floating iceberg.

Just make it through this one last show . . . One. Last. Time. And then you'll be free. I promise. I promise you that.

We'll both be free. We can both go home.

12

THE AUDIENCE SWEPT in a roar of applause and laughter, as he slurped the last of his drink then placed the empty cup on the floor by his feet. The man at the microphone removed his hat, bowed then bowed again, waved his arms in exaggerated gestures as he introduced the next performance in spectacular fashion: the amazing, the incredible, the uncanny . . . Tate the Elephant. *Tate!* He scooted forward in his seat, rubbed his hands together.

His eyes widened with excitement then narrowed into a glare as he watched that bastard, Lenny, walk onto the stage in his corny outfit waving a sparkly baton. Behind him, Tate hobbled up the ramp into the bright lights as hands clapped, as mouths cheered, as snares and cymbals clashed, as woodwinds and brass whistled and blared in an upbeat rhythm and melody unfitting to the atrocity occurring on stage, the cruel, demeaning, inhumane slave labor taking place. On Tate's head was a velvet hat with a twirled tassel, on his back draped fabric with a fancy embroidered design.

Clapping and cheering slowed then stopped altogether. The music came to a sudden and complete halt. On the stage was Lenny and his assistant, balls and rings in hand that they threw on the floor, each of them raising their hands. *What the—?* Now mumbling and whispers filled the strange silence. Tim could feel spectator heads turning and panning around, wondering if this was part of the show.

The assistant jerked in front with arms outstretched. Behind, Lenny raised the sparkly baton, shouted something. Tate backed up, in a sudden spurt, knocking Lenny backward onto the ground. His ears flared out. His trunk flailed up in the air, curled, side to side. The assistant jerked again, this time closer, and with this Tate rammed into him and pushed into the middle of the stage. There were gasps and outbursts of shock and disbelief in short snippets as Tate knocked the assistant down then around, like a dog playing with a rag doll, viciously mashing it, trying to tear out the stuffing.

Lenny appeared in front of Tate and held the baton up, stared him straight in the eye, shouted something else, motioned. Tate swayed on his legs, tail wagging behind him. Tim held a hand over his mouth as he watched, mouth agape, then put both hands on top his head. He could hear Tate breathing quick agitated breaths, starting to wheeze. He could see Tate gaze around, at each person in the stands, at Lenny, then around again. Tim noticed his eyes, wetter, blacker than he had ever seen. No more heads were turning. There was not a sound.

Tim stood to his feet, knocked over the empty cup, was about to yell something, then Tate charged forward, smashed Lenny down to the ground with his head, pressing in with enough force to collapse the entire stage. Tate then stomped down, hard, again and again, rolling him around and slid- ing him in violent bursts that stained the cream colored stage dark crimson—streaks and puddles and sprayed splatters. The spotlight dimmed, flashed on then off then back on, rattled, and went askew lighting the stage partway like an oblong crescent moon.

"TAAAAAAAATE!!!"

He yelled as loud as he could, one long shout that scraped the inside of his throat and strained the muscles on the sides of his neck, but couldn't hear his own voice. All around was an eruption of standing, clawing, rushing, screams and cries—more noise than could be deciphered, more motion than could be traced. Drowned out in the cacophony of chaos, he pushed towards the stage, but wedged between squirming bodies. A muffled voice announced over the speaker system that everyone should remain calm, that everything was under control. The words grew choppy and distorted with static, cutting out. Tim climbed on the seats, hopped up and down to see the stage. Tate moved in a circle, knocked equipment over, his front feet half-tangled in cables and cords.

Staff workers encircled the stage, rifles in hand. Guns raised, squinting down their sights, each took aim. Tim jumped down and squeezed through the crowd fleeing and panicking, shoving with urgency.

"Move! Move, god damn it! Get out the way!"

A grandmother led her granddaughter by the hand, a father held his children in his arms. Tim rammed through and about knocked them over.

"Get the fuck outta the way!!! Move it!" Tim continued to shove, nudging with his shoulders. "Move your fucking ass!"

The stage was empty, blood shining and starting to spill over the side. There was a tinge of something in the air, a peculiar smell. Tim heard a crash and some screaming behind him then turned. Tate galloped down the ramp and turned, smashed through a barrier towards the exit, sending a worker hurtling towards the wall and into a recycle bin. A table flipped over. Several people toppled to the floor as they scrambled to escape. Tim glanced again, staring at the bodies on stage: one with faint breathing that slowed, its limbs contorted at impossible angles, one completely still, its face a mangled mesh of flesh and bone.

He sprinted after Tate. As he passed, the worker moaned on the ground, clutching at his sides, every sound slurred with spittle and blood that foamed at his lips. One of the exit doors hung crooked, its hinge twisted and gnarled. The other lay on the ground in pieces. It was cold outside, dark. Along the wall were more injured, some hissing, some crying, some shouting for help. A woman lying sideways held her hands at the knee where something jagged stuck out, pleaded repeatedly in a stammered murmur to call the police, call the police . . .

Tim slowed to a side step, gazed at each horrified and pained face, turned around, watched as more ran towards the parking lot and into the streets. He jogged again then turned the corner, darting his head around, and at last found Tate pacing in the far corner. As he stepped close, he tried to calm his breathing and held a hand up.

"T-Tate . . . ?"

The elephant raised its head, hobbled over. Tim hugged at the leg, wrapped his arms around it tight, reached up and rubbed at the underbelly and up the side, feeling an object like a feathery stick jutting out. He removed it with a quick yank, then another that he threw down onto the ground with a slight chink. He could feel the animal shaking. The boy walked in front, touched the trunk, placed his palm on the forehead.

"You okay, boy?" Tim felt a strange sense of calm settle in. "It's okay . . . You're okay, boy . . . Everything's gonna be okay."

He panned around, took off the velvet hat, removed the draped fabric, tried to think as quick as he could. The circus grounds sprawled from the main building of the community center all the way to the park on the other side. *Damn it. That fence, remember.* The parking lot already started to jam up with honking and screeches. There was a crash then a loud clanging of metal. *Crap. Not much choice.* Tim put his hands on each side of Tate's head, stared him straight in the face.

"Tate, listen. We have got to go. We gotta run." He nodded along convincingly. "It's the only way, we have to. Have to."

13

It was getting darker. The boy tiptoed towards the parking lot, the elephant following with a heavy trot, using what little bushes, trees, pillars and telephone poles as cover. People shouted and pointed, running away. A car drove up over the median, tearing up the grass, then sped off. Tim dashed forward and led them into the streets in the quiet neighborhood. The ground vibrated with Tate's heavy stomps. Sliding into the intersection, he faced left then right, then went straight.

"Come on! Come on, boy!"

The commotion could still be heard as they pushed ahead, running straight in the middle of the street between parked cars. On either side were garages and driveways, windows lit up with families inside eating dinner and watching TV.

Tim faced up and noticed a little girl with her hands on the glass staring down, heard her call for Mommy to come look. He slipped on the hood of his hoodie then sped his jogging. They both continued forward in the blackening night, with each stomp's intensifying rattle. One of the car alarms almost set off. A flicker of the lights and a single loud honk, enough to make Tim's heart burst. He skidded on his heels, slapped his hands to his knees, gasping for air.

Ah, shit . . . Oh, man . . . What in the fuck.

Tate walked in a circle, pushing air out through his lips, making a low groaning noise. The streetlight illuminated their reflection in the window of a nearby truck. They appeared like monsters in a horror movie: eyes hollow and empty, faces sullen and gaunt from the mixture of light and shadow, bodies squished and stretched out from the curve of the glass.

Behind them in the darkness was a shriek from an open door. Driveways on either side started to light up, followed by random yells. They raced forward, cries echoing after them.

"Run, Tate!" Tim shifted back. "Run, boy, run!"

The elephant pulled in front. He glanced past scanning the houses behind. Another intersection ahead, Tim yelled to keep going, glanced back once more. As he turned to face forward, he was blinded by a brilliant flash of light. He covered his eyes, heard tires screech.

In the shining glow, the silhouette of a girl stood outside of a minivan, its door open. Her breathing rapid, shallow, she shivered then screamed. Reaching in her purse with shaky hands, she ran around to the back of the van, where she threw something. It bounced off of the animal's head with a thudded smack. Tate moved towards her, she moved away. They did this once more in a single counterclockwise turn, then again, circling, around, like a very dangerous game of Tag You're It.

"Tate!"

But it was already happening. The elephant chased the poor girl, dented the fender, banged the back bumper. The stomping, twisted metal and shrieks rang through the night air where a car alarm blared. Doors swung open. Windows slid up and down with heads popping out. Garage lights flicked on.

"No, Tate! Tate, stop!"

Tim watched the girl's face contort, her mouth open wide,

watched her desperately lunge, turn the corner about to be obliterated by the raging creature. He waved his arms, jumped up and down, but to no avail. Behind him, mixed with the headlights were intermittent haloes of red and blue. The hairs on his skin stiffened as he turned. The officer stepped out, raised his gun.

Bang, bang, bang, bang.

All he could see was a small flame like a candle burning sideways. All he could hear were slow screams from the girl and echoed stomps. There was a light smoky fume, then that same peculiar smell from back by the stage.

On the ground in front of him, the officer lay facedown in a puddle. His eyes shifted in and out of focus. The Glock trembled in his hands.

Another vehicle rolled in, this time the siren sounding. Tim aimed, pulled the trigger, watched the windshield crack. With a sudden sharp turn, it hopped up onto the curb pressing against a fire hydrant. Tate barreled towards it and rammed into its side, smashed down on it repeatedly. The hydrant burst open and fountained into the air in a crooked curve. He stared at the gun in his hand, blinked, tried to register what just happened, what he had just done. Behind him, the girl ran through the spraying water across a yard.

"Tate!"

He sprinted past the mashed-up cars and scattered debris, the elephant running alongside him. A helicopter whirred overhead, shining a bright light down over the glass shards, torn metal and splashing water, then the motionless body. An officer appeared from the shadows with a shotgun in both hands. Bang. Bang. Tim let Tate pass, watched the body fall backward, then ran again.

"Go, go!"

Spinning into the intersection, one from either side blocking them in, were the front ends of police vehicles that almost collided. Tim pointed the gun, pulled the trigger until there was a dull clicking noise. He knelt down, fumbled in his pocket for the other magazine. Tate bolted ahead. Officers stood behind the hood of each car: one on the left, two on the right. There was a loud trumpeting followed by a barrage of gunfire. Sliding the rack and chambering a round, he faced back up. Light from the helicopter hovered, gunshots flashed, then Tate's figure blurred back and forth. There was a rumbling in the ground.

Tim stood to his feet as another car drove past. Ahead, Tate stepped over a squishy torso and swung his head in a curved thrust tossing one of the officers into a side window. The car screeched to a halt, doors swinging open. Two officers stepped out and reached for their holsters until they each jerked, flinched, then toppled sideways. Tim jogged over, aiming the gun, fresh smoke wafting from the chamber block.

Blood dripped down Tate's ribs, some seeping out of his upper thigh. Across Tate's forehead and trunk were yellowish globs smeared with purple-black chunks. On Tim's neck and cheek was splattered blood, drippy and mixed with sweat. He gritted his teeth, tightened his grip, felt his arms shaking.

Sirens approached from every direction. In the distance, what appeared like Christmas lights twinkling glided along the horizon, closer and closer. Chopper blades above sent down gusts, shuffling hedge bushes and rattling tree branches, muting out all noise with the waves of rough wind.

Tim stared into Tate's eye, then reached out and touched him, shook his head as he stroked and petted. The animal groaned and nuzzled at his side.

"G-good boy, Tate . . ." He gulped. "You're such a good boy."

He shot at the first car, then the second, but as the convoy rushed in, they were surrounded. Tate rammed into one car then the other. Tim waited for the doors to open then shot at each one, turned, shot again, aimed, waited . . .

Boom!

It sounded like a bomb. It felt like a bomb. At first, before his brain could register, he thought it was an actual bomb.

Tim felt his body fly forward, felt his toes grind along the rocky surface. His body floated as he fell downward in mid-air in a belly flopping motion. There was red everywhere, like an explosion of confetti and streamers. The gun slipped from his fingers and tumbled away. He darted his eyes down the front of his hoodie—torn open like a busted piñata filled with raspberry jam. His lips oozed, his eyes glazed over. And then he slammed down hard on the concrete, heard a loud crack in his neck.

With a slow blink, he stared blankly ahead. A pool formed beneath his cheek and spilled in front of him where a foot stepped near. His limbs were numb, he couldn't move, and his lids drooped.

Tate . . .

Run away, Tate . . .

Officers crept forward, weapons in hand, like a pack of wolves. One of them nudged the boy on the ground with his shoe, then shook his head. With its ears out, tail wagging, and trunk straight down, the elephant watched the circle shrink around it. A flashlight from one of the guns shined on the big black eye.

There was a trumpeting roar as the creature rose then crashed back down and plowed into them. Two officers were flung, one of them trampled. Some jumped out of the way, others began to open fire in a scrambled frenzy. The elephant rammed one of them forward into a car, knocking it over on its side, then turned around and crushed a whole line of them in a row—mixed shouting and splats, rumbled stamping and crashing.

Walkie-talkies cut in and out, radios from inside cars squeaked and crackled. Shots continued, and the animal began to slow down, grew more clumsy and weak. Its breaths grew heavy. Blood covered its skin and sopped to the ground.

A few officers remained. The rest were on the ground, lifeless or incapacitated. They in turn cocked their weapons, reloaded new magazines, took aim and fired in sporadic bursts. One of them struggled to reset his rifle that jammed, a spent shell stuck in the chamber. The elephant galloped over, banged him and stomped down, with just a sliver of the ferocity from before. The others fired with increased intensity as each crushing blow turned his yelling into squealing, a muffled murmur, then one last wheezing breath.

The elephant turned away with a wobbly limp, waddled, then leaned against the side of a jeep. Firing slowed as it slid down to the ground. One of the officers motioned, and the others lowered their weapons. The man knelt, nudged the glasses to the crook of his nose, watched the elephant's eye that was weeping.

"Oh, God, what have we done . . ."

"I know."

"No choice. Sedatives weren't working."

The man stood again, turned toward the others, their pale horrified faces. He shifted back to the animal on the ground. Its eye wept steady, rolled up and back. He reluctantly raised his weapon.

"It's suffering . . ."

"Jesus."

Around them, bodies sprawled: some facedown, some twisted and rolled on their sides. There were puddles and smeared bits and pieces clinging to the concrete.

The man removed his glasses, dabbed fingers over his eyes, then fumbled to put them back on.

"Come on, guys."

The crowd that gathered was silent and still, except for whimpers and sobs. A single reporter took her place at the far front of the scene, adjusted her blouse, then gazed into the camera lens. She stared for a moment, a gloom in her eyes as the final gunshots sounded. Then, she held the microphone, cleared her throat, and began speaking.

14

THE THOMPSON CIRCLE Incident, as it became known, was a lightning rod of controversy. Animal rights activists and youth advocates were outraged, demanded changes in legislation. Government officials defended the actions of local authorities, stated appropriate measures were being taken. Eyewitness accounts of the events were released through the media. National figures commented on the tragedy, expressed their deepest sympathies to the families of those that were injured or killed. Children and families gathered on the street where the elephant and the boy had died. Letters, cards, drawings, flowers, candles and toys littered the area where a sign was posted.

END THE ABUSE
END THE KILLING

It took a single shot to take down ten-year-old Tim. Ninety-eight shots were used to stop Tate—the amazing, the incredible, the uncanny . . . Tate the Elephant.

HEMINGWAY DORKS AND THE JURASSIC ROCK

1

THE FIRST MOVIE I ever watched in theaters was *Jurassic Park*. I remember it was me and my little brother, my mom and dad, a bag of popcorn, and a couple of sodas. And it was the awesomest thing I'd ever seen, I'd ever experienced. It had a lasting impression on me: I wanted to be a paleontologist, just like Dr. Grant. I used to go to the library at school, look up books on reptiles and amphibians, on dinosaurs, on paleontology and geology, on all things paleozoic era. I was pretty much obsessed. So it would come as no surprise that when I was playing in the field at recess, and tripped on a rock, that I immediately concluded it was a fossil—a dinosaur bone.

It was 1994-1995 (you know how the school year is counted) and I was in fifth grade. I had a *Jurassic Park* folder, a *Jurassic Park* wristwatch, *Jurassic Park* pencils, everything except a *Jurassic Park* lunch box. I even had the action figures at home: a Dr. Grant, a Tim and a Muldoon, and of course, a whole plethora of dinosaurs. I remember I used to order books from like the Scholastic catalog, even. Yeah . . . Jack Horner, eat your heart out. That's the expert that they used for the movie.

My two best friends were Mark and Jared, and we used

to play by this one big tree. We would play like *Power Rangers* or *Aliens* or some other silly thing that involved kicking and screaming and running around at/from something make-believe. Yeah, those were the good ol' days. One recess, while trying to show off my roundhouse kick à la Jean-Claude Van Damme, I ended up tripping on this enormous rock. I glanced down at it, astonished, mesmerized, then glanced up at my two friends, eyes wide, mouth open.

"Guys . . . Guys, guys!"

"What?" They ran over to me, smelly and sweating. "What is it?"

"Holy cow. Look at that." I turned to one of them, then the other. "That, my friends, is a freaking *dinosaur* bone."

"Oh, shoot. Really?"

"Yeah, really. Look at it!"

"Y'know . . . it does kinda look like it."

I stooped down on one knee, wiped some of the dirt off of it. "No, see. The way it curves, this is the jawbone of a velociraptor."

"Wow." They both nodded, arms crossed. "Okay, so let's get back to it. You just changed from green ranger to white—"

"No, you guys!"

Tilting their heads, they stared at me with grimaced faces.

"Don't you see? We have to uncover this. Come on, this could be the discovery of all frickin' time."

2

AND SO THE excavation began. Each and every day—before, during and after school, mostly at recess—we would find the biggest and strongest twigs and branches, use smaller rocks as chisels not unlike our caveman ancestors, and dig and dig. We even tried using rulers and mechanical pencils but they always broke, then our parents would get mad. As the piles of dirt began to shift around, and clouds of dust began to blow, some of the other kids would walk by and be like, what the hell is that? And so they, too, joined in.

It was quite a wondrous sight to behold: geeks, cool kids, special ed, bullies, boys, girls, cooties, someone's pet chameleon, working together, side by side. The rock now had a fairly significant moat dug around it and it was starting to reveal its true form . . . which, sad to say, was starting to not appear like a velociraptor after all.

Aw, crud. I don't know about this . . .

But it was too late now. There was no stopping this angry lynch mob dead set on digging up this boulder, this meteor, this whopping chunk of earth. Some of them would grit their teeth, moan and groan and grunt as they pelted, pounded away, pulled out loose wads of red dirt that stained their clothes and clung to the sweat on their skin. It was getting a little intense, a little bit insane even.

Nobody cared, though. It wasn't even about "dinosaurs" anymore. *There weren't even dinosaurs* on *this island!* I later thought but told no one. What we all knew, but nobody ever said aloud, was that this thing was something so much more . . . that this was something we all *had* to do . . . that this thing had been waiting for us our entire lives, maybe even longer than that.

When the sad day came that our teacher found out, caught us red-dirt-handed and shut down the operation, we all felt a sadness sink within us—for we knew that it was something we couldn't and shouldn't give up on, no matter what.

Each kid dispersed one by one, leaving the scene of the crime. Jared shifted back. Mark tugged at my arm, but I wouldn't budge.

"Come on, man. We gotta go."

"No . . ."

"It's over. Sorry."

I gazed down at the half-uncovered rock, almost two-thirds already. I clenched my fists at my sides, turned to face the crowd that was walking away.

"No, we can't just stop!"

"But Mrs. Nelson—"

"To hell! With Mrs. Nelson!!!"

There were gasps and subsequent whispers. The crowd now watched me, engaged, silent. Nobody said a thing, nobody moved an inch.

After the longest awkward pause, this one kid teetered forward. He was using crutches, had his foot in a cast, and hobbled forth until he stood right next to me, balancing the devices at his armpits.

Jared stepped with arms crossed, nodded, then faced the group too. Mark shook his head then reluctantly followed, adjusting his glasses, putting a hand on my shoulder.

All the other kids came back, one after the other, like we were playing Follow the Leader. I knelt down, and so did they, listening intently.

"Okay . . ." I stared each and every one of them in the eye, with the utmost seriousness, like we were about to go to war. "Here's what we're gonna do . . ."

I took a branch dang near worn down to the nub from our stash of supplies at the base of the tree, began to draw in the dirt laying out the new plan. As we huddled together in the shade, surrounding the fat rock half-sticking up outta the ground, something changed, and the whole shenanigan made a lot of sense.

3

THIS WAS FIFTH grade, our last year in elementary. Next year, we would all be off to intermediate school, and then everything would be different. Soon it would be sex ed and pimples and who-likes-who. It was *our* time now. No, this rock was not just a freaking rock, it was the symbol of our impending adolescence—and it was bursting forth, wanting to be let free. And that was just what we intended to do.

The master plan went as follows: the smart girls who sat at the front of the class would bug the teach with questions about our science project (some lima bean or something) as long as they could, the delinquents in trouble would clap the chalk erasers by the fence so as to give us some cloud cover, the hopscotchers would keep watch since they would be right outside the door, the hopscotchers would try to block and signal the kids on the swings, the kids on the swings would jump off and kick a kickball in our direction, then the rest of us would scatter. Fool. Proof.

Our first attempt ended up with Mark getting beamed in the face, every indentation from the surface of the ball etched in his cheek, along with the word Spalding written backwards.

Poor guy didn't even see it coming. But hey, the causalities of war.

We kept at it—some days we were able to get an inch deeper, some days just a centimeter, other days a centimeter came back up from the wind or rain—until, at last, we got the dang thing exposed. Overheated, exhausted, we plopped down onto the grass, the dirt, the mud, and the gravel. As we lay there catching our breath, some of us wiping the sweat from our brow, hopelessly peering at the water fountain all the way over by the playground, one thought went through all our heads.

If only we could . . . pull that thing outta there . . . this would all be over . . .

Mark sat up, adjusted his glasses now taped in the middle. The kid with crutches leaned on one, hyperventilated. Jared rolled onto his side, mumbled to himself, began to stagger to his feet. So did everyone else. I lay there a second longer, slimy from sweat, burning up, a heavy thumping in my chest, as a hand hovered over my face. One of the other kids—I don't know who, didn't know him—helped me back up.

I put a hand on Jared's shoulder, put an arm around Mark, faced the kid in crutches, faced the kid with the chameleon, faced each kid drenched in sweat, their clothes smeared with dirt and mud, random sticks and stones at their feet. A kid nodded, then another then another. Until all at once, in unison, we turned and knelt down over the big hole, placed our hands on the gigantic rock. We pulled on it, at first in different directions, going against each other, then synced our efforts and slammed it hard into the side wall, began to roll it upwards, lift it. It was a tug of war against gravity, against the very planet itself.

Heave! *Heeeave!!!*

It was a miracle. The round, misshapen object tumbled along the rim of the edge, and flipped onto the ground with a loud thud. We all stood back, in disbelief, and before we could even comprehend what had just taken place, there was a loud rumbling sound all around us.

The kids on the swing jumped off, watched in horror—

The hopscotchers stopped in place—

The delinquents stared, jaw-dropped, chalk erasers in each hand—

The smart girls popped their heads outta the classroom, dropped a few lima beans—

The teacher ran over, hysterical, flailing her arms about—

Above us, branches began to rattle and shake. In front, the trunk began to sway and lean, began to slip into the empty hole, then crashed diagonally into the rock. We gazed at it all, astonished, mesmerized. It was the coolest thing we'd ever seen, we'd ever experienced. The fallen tree. The deep and wide hole. The rock above ground, which did turn out to be just a dang rock. One of the bullies held a hand up, I slapped him a high five. One of the smart girls ran up and kissed me on the cheek, I reddened with a blush.

We all got detention, of course. No one as long as me. They forced me to do push-ups and write lines repeatedly, over and over again, until my hand hurt. And, you know what, it was so freaking worth it. Even then, in the counselor's office, as I sat there staring at the piece of paper filled with wavy columns of words, I had a great big smile on my stupid face. Know why? Because—every letter, every word, every sentence, every page, every minute, every hour, every day, every week—I had my *Jurassic Park* folder and my *Jurassic Park* wristwatch and my *Jurassic Park* pencil. I was Dr. Grant on that little desk in that little room.

REACH FOR NEW HEIGHTS

1

ONLY A FOOL climbs Mount Akaiwa twice, a saying in Japanese I never heard of but soon would know all too well. A fool indeed, as I slipped into my baggy jeans, kicked on my skater shoes and threw on my hoodie. It had a beige skull design across the front with fur lining along the hood. Glancing around the studio, I snatched the backpack from the chair, grabbed my composition book. On the futon was my cell phone, which I bent down to pick up. Battery half-dead, wallpaper background dim, I couldn't help but smile at her smiling back. My girl. I missed her, and I couldn't wait to see her again.

The park I was supposed to meet Nilesh was just a few blocks away so I walked it. I was early, and my friend was always late, which meant I could take my time. Nice and cool out, I could hear cicadas in the distance. I circled around the pond, gazed at the pads rippling on the surface of the water, sat down on a rock. A small bridge hovered across with a crane perched on the side. I took my phone out again, stared at her—at her eyes, at her lips—thought about her body waiting for me back home. I sighed, then twisted the promise ring on my finger.

"Um . . . What the hell ya doin', mate?"

"Huh?" I faced up, put the phone back in my pocket. "Oh, hey."

"Where's your waterproof clothes?"

"Waterproof . . . clothes?"

"Yeah." He shook his head, shifted with a crooked smile. "Two people died last week of hypothermia."

"Two people what—?"

He went on to explain the news report of two poor souls that got caught in the rain on the slopes, their body temperature dropping to fatal levels. I stared in response. Poking the glasses back to the crook of his nose, he tugged on the strap of his duffel bag, then zipped up his bright red jacket.

"And how high is this mountain???"

"Ya serious?" Nilesh couldn't help but smile again. "About four thousand meters, give or take. Under fourteen thousand feet."

"Oh, shit . . ."

"Come then. We'd better go and visit the konbini, at least nab a couple things before we meet the others."

The doors slid open as we stepped out onto the platform along with the crowd, walking past pillars on either side and down a set of stairs. Recorded announcements played over the speaker system, followed by beeping and chimes. We stood out since we were foreigners, not to mention we had on all this funny gear. Well, he did. I was dressed normal.

"I can't believe . . ." Nilesh shook his head again with that crooked smile. "Mate . . ."

"Okay." I let him have his moment, deservedly so. "C'mon, man."

"Haha. Fair enough."

Passersby stepped up and up as we filed in after, taking a swift right to a small convenience store, or konbini, located there in the station. Most train stations did have a konbini, and maybe a bakery, plus a line of vending machines.

"And how we feelin'?"

"Whatchu mean?"

"Well. You're about to leave Japan soon. Are you excited? Are ya ready? Scaling a mountain with zero prep is one gutsy way to go, for sure."

I smirked back, watched as he grabbed item after item from the shelves.

"Let's see. Ah, yes."

"I wish things worked out here . . ."

I trailed off then, drifting away in my mind. Thinking about leaving this place I've come to love, and thinking about going back home to the states.

He said something but I didn't catch it. I nodded anyway, as I twisted the promise ring on my finger. I was technically standing there next to him, technically in that store, in that station, but I was elsewhere at the same time.

2

Daydreaming, still lost in thought, worried, Nilesh nudged me on the shoulder in the back seat. We had arrived at the foot of the mountain. It was a good three-and-a-half hour drive from the far side of the neighboring prefecture. First we met by train, then rented a car. The others each got out and circled around to gather their things. I never met them 'til that day, both friends of Nilesh. I followed, gazing up, attempting to get one good glimpse but it was too large to see all at once.

Ah, so this is it. The infamous Mount Akaiwa.

They took their time pulling out fancy tools and equipment, stuffing thick rucksacks and fastening heavy cleated boots. I grabbed my practically empty backpack. I unzipped and made sure everything was there: a generic emergency rain poncho, a dinky flashlight keychain, my composition book, some snacks, and a couple bottles of water. It was pretty much whatever our last minute stop at the konbini could provide.

Each of them began to stretch, which I mimicked, feeling inadequate in comparison. *Maybe this wasn't such a great idea after all . . . Spider-sense tingling . . .* Not gonna lie, I was getting tired just stretching.

The start of the Gotemba path was pretty flat. Nilesh

walked near me while the other two took the front. I dragged my feet, hung my head down low. Glancing out over the ledge, I could see a vast silver lake beyond thick forest with cities in the distance beyond that. I stopped in place, admiring the pristine majestic view.

"You awright, mate?"

"Fan-freaking-tastic."

"I reckon you regret coming?"

"Nah, I just feel kinda like underprepared or something. I show up in skater shoes while these guys come in here looking like they're about to hurl a ring into Mordor."

I crossed my arms as Nilesh snickered at this.

"Seriously, though, look at 'im. What is up with that guy?"

"Ah, well, he's a proper veteran climber. Done this kind of thing quite a lot. Cy, our de facto fearless leader."

"Hmm." I glared at his back, tall and slender. "And what about the other one, your friend? He a badass, too?"

"Yūhi, he works at my school. Just a normal bloke." He reached back and pulled out his canteen, sipped. "I mean, he does play tennis so he's pretty fit."

"So . . . I got skater shoes on, have never done this before, *and* I'm the most outta shape. Great."

3

LIKE I SAID, the start of the Gotemba path was pretty flat, but that soon changed. The two others were way in front now, almost out of sight, Nilesh was in the middle, and an ever-widening gap grew between the group and myself. I slipped further and further back with each wobbly step. After about fifteen minutes at a constant forty-five degree angle, I plopped down on a nearby rock with my face between my knees. Nilesh placed a hand on my back as I wiped the sweat from my brow, breathing heavy exerted breaths.

"You go on. Will catch up," I heard Cy say.

I arched my head back in agony, squinting up at the sun. Nilesh turned to him, then turned at me, back to him. Cy lay his rucksack down and nodded.

Why'd you come back this way . . .

It annoyed me he had gone through the extra effort and still appeared so comfortable and relaxed.

"Uh, you do know this is the 'easy' part, right?"

I peered sideways at him as he took out a Nikon camera. He adjusted the barrel of the lens, tilted it and poked at the screen.

"I . . . I don't know if I can do this."

"Well, that's up to you. Not too late to turn back, maybe just stay behind. Better sooner rather than later, eh, if I can be honest." He aimed, snapped a quick shot. "God. Beautiful, isn't she?"

The reflection of the sun shimmered on the surface of the lake like molten lava. It was spectacular.

"All right, then, Mister Fearless Leader, what exactly is the plan here?"

He grinned, knelt down and started digging through his pack. "So. Not turning around, then?"

"Nah, I guess not just yet."

"Good on ya." Standing back up, he unfolded a walking stick and held it out to me. "And there we are."

"This gonna help?"

He nodded, pulling his rucksack on. I turned it over in my hand, examined it, then stabbed it into the dirt, hobbling up.

"Well then. Shall we?"

Cy led the way and I followed, my limbs already starting to feel heavy again.

"It's going to be about this steep from here on. Once you push past the barrier, the pain, the fatigue, it should get easier."

He glanced back, walking with apparent ease.

"Use the rocks stuck in the dirt for your stepping. Switch hands when holding the stick now and again to even out the load. Maintain three points of contact, especially when it gets slippy."

"Like this?"

"Uh . . ."

It was pretty lame, but it was sound advice. Carefully stepping from each patch of stuck rock to the next did help give a better grip. I could feel the difference.

"There's a cabin we need to get to before dark. We'll rest

there, wake up early, and climb again. We should hit the peak at sunrise tomorrow."

I didn't realize it was going to take so long. It was almost mid-afternoon, and we had just begun. Maybe I should've called her before I left, or at least sent her a text. I took my phone out. No reception. I stopped in place, twisted at the ring.

"You okay?"

"Yeah. Yeah, I'm fine."

4

THE SUN OVERHEAD was relentless, my muscles ached, and I was out of breath. I must have taken ten rest breaks since the last two rest breaks. I could tell the others were already getting tired of me dragging so hard. Nilesh came and sat down by me, yet again. Yūhi paused midway between us and Cy, staring back with a hand on his hip. Cy was already way up high, almost around the bend.

Hand on my shoulder, Nilesh bent over. I couldn't see his eyes but I could see his pointy nose and teeth and chin. "Mate?"

"I . . . I'm . . ." I said between breaths, my head bobbing up and down. "I am getting . . . to the top . . . top of this *fucking* mountain . . ." I could see his lips curl into a smile. "Even if it takes me a million, bajillion god damn rest breaks."

Nilesh helped me up and we caught up to Yūhi who had his back turned, crouched on the ground. In his hands was an iPod with a mini-speaker attached. I started singing along as we drew closer, even with my shallow breathlessness.

"You know song?" His eyes were wide.

"Oh, yeah. Of course," I said back. "One of my faves."

"Very good taste in music." His accent was pretty thick,

almost sounded like *berry* good. He laughed then turned it up louder.

The three of us fettered back up the ascent to Cy, in a line single form, to the sound of Asian Kung-Fu Generation.

❧

We were like a trail of ants marching: our fearless leader on ahead out of eyeshot, two of us taking up the middle, and me lagging behind. The sun hid behind cloud now while a steady gust blew upon us. I put my hood up. Cy slipped on a beanie. Nilesh blew into cupped hands. Yūhi tightened the scarf around his neck. I could feel the dirt slide and roll beneath my feet just the slightest bit.

I stopped in place, admired the tranquil beauty below. It seemed like a good opportunity to catch my breath and have a quick drink. Even though it was getting cooler, our leader said to keep hydrating.

Ah. I wish you were here.

Nilesh also saw the opportunity, crept behind a rock and relieved himself. He adjusted as the stream formed into a puddle between his feet. Yūhi happened to glance back, flinched in a double take, turned away and shuffled through songs on his iPod. I couldn't help but laugh to myself.

That was when we heard the shout. That was when we saw the puff of dust, the rocks and pebbles tumbling.

Cy!!!

Before this particular moment that would be the beginning of our impending ordeal, we were just four guys on a mountain. Four idiots. Four . . . fools.

"Shit! Go, go!" I shoved Nilesh, who hurried to zip up about to fall down behind me. "Hurry up, c'mon!"

Yūhi waved us up then turned and leapt. "Hayaku!"

Either we had taken too long a break, Cy pulled ahead just that much, or the bend was steep enough and at such an angle that he disappeared from our view. Perhaps all the above. A cold sweat and tingling numbness sank down my skin to my body as I pulled alongside Yūhi. He hopped from rock to rock and I scrambled using the walking stick in almost a gallop. Nilesh fell behind, almost crawling in desperation.

Me and Yūhi turned and about slipped ourselves. We saw Cy's beanie on the ground covered in red dirt. Our jaws dropped as we stared over the edge. *No . . . No, it can't be . . .* It was eerily quiet and still then. I was ready to drop to a knee to peek over the side. That was when we heard it again, saw it again. The shouting. The dust.

Behind us, to the left, Cy writhed on the ground.

5

ONE BY ONE, we huddled around the poor bastard holding his ankle, rocking side to side on the dirt. His face was contorted in a grimace as he hissed and winced, eyes darting at each of us. Nilesh stepped forward first, placed his hand on Cy's shoulder. Then Yūhi knelt down with his hands on his knees, mouth agape.

"Blimey! I twisted my *bloody* fucking ankle! Bollocks."

"Wha . . . What do we do?" I asked.

That eerie quiet, that eerie stillness set in again. Around us, there was miles and miles of open air, high up there in the sky. I hadn't noticed 'til then how we were so close to the very clouds, almost like we were in a mist or fog.

"R-reach into my pack, will ya." Cy was fidgeting.

Nilesh grabbed the rucksack, searched inside.

"Will need to do a proper wrapping."

Yūhi glanced over at me, and I glanced back. Then Cy's eyes and mine locked for a split second before he turned again to his foot.

Nilesh pulled out a roll of brown gauze, held it up.

"Good, good. Got anything hard?"

As Nilesh began to search again, I fumbled through and took out my composition book.

"That'll do, thanks very much. 'Preciate it." He tore off the cover, ripped it in half, and placed a half on either side. I knelt down and held them in place while he wrapped from the heel up to the mid-shin.

Our eyes locked again, and he nodded. I handed the walking stick back, which he used to stagger up. I stood along with him.

"Very well. What we standing 'round for?"

He stepped past, with a noticeable limp.

"Wait. Cy, you're bleeding, shouldn't we—" I tried to say.

"No."

"Cy—" Nilesh tried to second.

"No." He shifted, just a little, enough to reveal the corner of his eye as he leaned on the stick. "No, I said."

The three of us turned to one another not saying a word, watching as he continued back up on the path with that limp, limp, limp . . .

One man down.

6

We were moving at a far slower pace. The sun pelting down pierced through the haze that started to creep in and cover us all. It was an odd warmth, even with the clouds. Perhaps we had just been at this for a while now. A light mist of cloud washed over us, as we shambled up the mountain like decaying undead.

Me and Yūhi were in front, continuing our rock playlist on the iPod mini-speaker. In the middle was Cy limping away. And a little further down, Nilesh was a mere splash of bright red amongst the gravel terrain.

I scanned down, shouted. "Everybody okay!?"

The sound was both an echo yet hollow at the same time, in that space between us.

"Never! Better!!!" I heard Cy shout back with a slight delay.

I cupped a hand to block out the sun, saw Nilesh hold up one of his arms in what I assumed was either a thumbs up or an all-okay.

Things became pretty quiet then, as we all focused on climbing, watching our steps. I remembered to keep sipping even though I wasn't thirsty. Cy said, by the time your lips become dry, it's too late. I was still taking breaks, but somehow managed to keep ahead with Yūhi. I guess that wasn't surprising as our de facto leader did have the limp and all.

It was clear when we first hit the slopes, a vibrant blue that stretched on past the city and forests below, the lake appearing like a perfect mirror reflection. Now, though, it was starting to become pure white as we walked through cloud.

Quite an interesting thing, new and surreal, I had never experienced that before. Almost like being in a dream or disappearing away in slow motion.

This is so cool . . . Woow.

It was kinda fun, like playing in the snow or something. I couldn't help but smile, a warm fuzzy feeling welling up inside me. Staring at my outstretched hand no longer opaque, I moved my fingers open and closed, glancing down at my body and feet that were equally blotted out with white.

I turned back to make sure everyone was still okay. I could just make them out but Cy continued his steady hobble, and beneath him that bright red-orange speck that was Nilesh glided along. When I faced back up, I saw Yūhi spinning the dial of the iPod. Then I touched my ring.

Ah, wish you could see this. It's so beautiful.

Yūhi pulled ahead a little bit, and I could still hear the faint music. I saw him readjust the scarf around his neck. I tightened the hoodie snug against my ears and jaw and let the drawstring float and twirl in the increasing wind. It started to cool off as the clear vibrant blue fading to white now turned gray as dusk descended upon us.

Over his shoulder, Yūhi turned back and shouted. "Ah, I see!"

I gazed to where he pointed—it was still far up, but the

dilapidated wooden shed was like heaven compared to the whitish gray haze. Cy laughed triumphantly, raising both hands in the air.

I smiled, glancing past him at Nilesh, who had a hand over his face and seemed to be stumbling. Yūhi was already double timing it to the cabin. Cy was way too happy to notice. I tossed my bag on the ground and started back down.

"Where we off to? Cabin's up there!"

"I'm gonna wait for Nilesh."

He nodded and limped past. As I made my way down step by step, carefully chose my footing, I could see Nilesh was in some sort of trouble, struggling. He appeared disoriented.

"Nilesh!" I almost tripped. "Nilesh!!!"

I got up close and caught him just in time as he was about to fall onto a jagged rock. "Nilesh, what's the matter?"

"I've got quite a rather bad headache," he said. "I'm burnin' up, mate."

I put my hand on his cheek then his forehead but couldn't tell since my hands were frozen. Behind me, Yūhi made his way towards us.

"Doushita no? Nilesh-san?"

"I don't know . . ." I tossed his duffel bag, which Yūhi caught. "Get to the cabin, I got 'im."

I wrapped my arm around his waist and propped his arm on my neck.

"The hut, it's right there."

He swallowed, nodded, eyes closed now. I struggled to shift his weight with mine, pulling the two of us along. The wind started to blow a little harder.

Yūhi stopped and was breathing heavy, let us pass as he pointed, then dragged the heavy pack across the dirt as his arms were getting tired. He also snatched up my bag. My bag on his back was pretty light in comparison since it was practically empty.

I could see Cy hold the door open, waiting. I never seen him worried 'til then.

"Come on, lads!"

Standing in place, my muscles were already shaking. Yūhi caught up and stopped too.

"Tsukareta . . ."

"Me too. One last bit. Can you make it, Nilesh?" This time he didn't nod. "Shit . . ."

As we made our way, his head started to hang down and his legs grew increasingly unsteady. *Almost there. Just a little further.* We squeezed into the doorway and sprawled on the floor as Cy slammed the door shut. He mumbled a prayer of thanks and knelt down near us.

"Bloody 'ell." He unzipped Nilesh's jacket, opened it a little, pouring some water on his head, took off his glasses. "This could be heat stroke. You been drinking?"

Nilesh didn't respond.

I watched sideways from the floor, holding my side that throbbed. Yūhi struggled to breathe as he lay on his back.

"You needn't worry. Will rest here."

Two men down.

7

CY WRAPPED A blanket around Nilesh who was starting to feel a little better, touched his forehead and gave him an encouraging grin. He then rolled back over and adjusted the wrapping on his ankle. I glanced at the two of them then stared out the window at the darkness. Was all this really happening or perhaps a lucid dream unfolding?

"Sorry, mate . . ." His voice was almost a whisper.

"That's okay, Nilesh. Just glad you're all right."

"You know the saying?"

We both shifted back to Cy who tightened the gauze with one final tug.

"They say, 'Only a fool climbs Mount Akaiwa twice.' And hell if that isn't spot-on, huh."

Head on my backpack, I curled into a little shrimp ball on my side hugging myself in the fetal position. The konbini didn't have blankets. I turned the other way, faced Yūhi. "Hey, why don't you play some Pillows while we sleep?"

"Ha, very good choice."

Cy had his face nestled between his pack and the floor, studying the map. I could hear the crinkle from the paper as he turned it sideways one way then the other. We all lay there, quiet, in kind of a diamond shape.

I pulled my phone out, stared at her face and smiled. I stared at her lips, her eyes, thought about her body—thought about how earlier I wished she was here, but now was so glad she wasn't. What a freaking disaster.

Just then, the little icon in the corner turned red. The battery was about to die.

❦

I watched until the red bar shrank, began to blink, then shut off. My eyelids started to fall but I fought to try to remain awake. I lingered on the blank screen for a good long while then I must have given in and fallen asleep 'cause Yūhi teased me when he shook me back awake. I shuddered, took a second to realize where I was.

"Why you snore? So loud."

It was even darker out, even colder. Nilesh was eating some fruit, Cy had a half-eaten sandwich in his hand. I took out and slurped on one of my energy gel packs. I was starting to sniffle. Yūhi popped the last of his cone sushi into his mouth.

"All right, gents. We best leave soon if we're to make the summit by sunup. It is going to be cold, and chances are it will likely rain."

I took out the rain poncho Nilesh grabbed for me at the konbini. He glanced over and nodded. I slid it on over my hoodie, the extra layer helping to keep me warm.

They started to stretch again which I copied.

And, here, we, go . . .

"Can you imagine building this thing way out here? It has got to have some kind of Buddhist meaning or something," Nilesh said.

We all turned to Yūhi who shrugged.

"I'm just glad it's here."

"Same."

Nilesh zipped up his jacket then rubbed his hands together. Cy slipped on his beanie, pulled his rucksack on. Yūhi put on his scarf.

Cy was the first one to step out, limp still present but a little better. He held the door open. "Torches on."

I didn't immediately recognize what he meant at first. *Oh, torches . . .* Yūhi had a very strong flashlight that pierced the darkness like a lightsaber. Nilesh had one that he strapped around his head, as did Cy. There I was with my dinky key-chain version, and it just lit up the small space in front of me.

8

BEFORE, IT WAS serene and tranquil, so beautiful, with the lake below, the forests stretching on and on into the distance, and the mystical layer of cloud. Now it was pitch black out. You almost couldn't make out your footing, even with torches up and what little sheen from the moon looming behind the blanketed sky.

Cy was in the lead, me behind, and Nilesh and Yūhi together in back. I kept up with him a lot easier than I did before. I wasn't out of breath, I didn't need a rest break.

"Good stepping. A second wind, perhaps. Well done." It felt good to hear him say that since I was by far the weakest link in the chain.

He let me pull in front, let the other two pass as well, then took up the rear.

Raindrops started to fall in teeny-tiny splits and splats on the rocky surface. I felt some of my steps slide as I zigzagged. We stayed huddled closer together this time: me, then Yūhi, Nilesh, and then Cy. I chose the route, picked each step carefully in the dim light.

This drizzle was different from the cloud fog-mist. It was

a spritz that hit you like a thousand tiny spikes. It hurt 'cause of its velocity, but it also hurt 'cause it was so damned cold.

My nose sniffled. "It's fucking freezing out here."

I could hear mumbled agreement behind me.

Out of nowhere, my skater shoe slipped off a rounded rock and I was about to go down hard to the ground but Yūhi caught me in time.

"Thank—" I turned to face him, quick, caught my breath. "I mean, arigatou."

"Betsu ni." He breathed too. "Very danger."

Very danger, indeed.

We continued our ascent, in the cold, in the damp dark. Nobody talked or joked now. There was no rock music on an iPod mini-speaker. Nothing. I couldn't feel my fingers or face, and my nose continually dripped, straight from my nostrils to the ground as if it were a leaky faucet. It felt like I was blinking a lot slower too.

The sun pierced the horizon, stretching bright orange against dark purple, otherworldly silver-gold and indigo. I twirled the promise ring on my finger.

"Look, the sun starting to come up."

"Ah. Yes, but there's still time before the actual sunrise. In fact, we better double up pace if we're gonna make it."

Cy turned to the others who nodded.

Me and Cy climbed side by side. It was starting to become easier to see again.

I wasn't paying as much attention to my footing, I was more mesmerized by the colors around and beneath us. Dirt and rocks were washed over first by fluffy cloud then were lost in the darkness, but now was an ephemeral oil-and-water puddle that exploded into a rainbow.

Absolutely amazing . . . This is . . .

I couldn't quite find the words, even in my own head. It surpassed all logic or explanation. It was aesthetic beauty in its most pure form, aligned in a perfectly timed moment, somehow fleeting.

For the first time through the whole ordeal, I felt so appreciative to be there way up high. Then, on that mountain, with three of the finest. Gazing down from atop, from afar, at where it wasn't clear where the earth began and the heavens ceased.

A thing like that makes you feel so tiny.

A thing like that makes you forget everything else.

A thing like that changes you.

"Fellas, wait . . ."

I lingered there a moment, turned off my light then turned back. Nilesh and Cy were huddled around Yūhi who leaned back on the ground.

Three men down.

9

It had stopped raining but the ground was still slick as I made my way to the group. My heart thumped in my chest. Goosebumps raised on my forearms. Cy leaned on the walking stick, Nilesh was on his knees with a hand on Yūhi. I almost slipped but caught my balance, closing the gap between me and the others.

"Damn, so close."

"He vomited, and he's having trouble breathing." Nilesh glanced up at me.

"W-what do we—"

"It's altitude sickness. Only option's to descend." Cy shook his head, turned away. "It is absolutely necess'ry."

"Like you said, we're so close, is there—"

"No. He won't get better. The only way now is back down." Cy looked me straight in the eye. "Mountain like this, sometimes people bring little tanks of oxygen."

I was quiet, wiped my nose with my sleeve. "How's your head, Nilesh?"

"Still pounding, mate."

"And how 'bout the ankle?"

"Not a problem." Although his limp said otherwise.

I stepped closer to Yūhi, who seemed to dry heave a little bit. "Yūhi . . ."

He turned to throw up, but just a bit of water and spittle came out. It was dry heaving, obviously painful from the way he groaned.

"I'm okay. I—"

Tongue out, eyes bulged, his face reminded me of a fish that had been yanked from the ocean, struggling to breathe.

"No. See, we have to go back."

"Shame. We're so close to the top. And the sunrise . . ." Nilesh said.

"Okay, let's get him back down. It's over." I went on the other side of Nilesh and we helped him to his feet.

"Ah . . . Thank you . . ." His accent came through again.

"Wait."

Me and Nilesh turned, Yūhi with an arm around each of us.

"I have to keep going. I just have to."

"But Cy—"

"I know but . . ." He shook his head.

I bit my bottom lip, shook my head too. "Damn it. Nilesh, you got him?"

"Yeah. I got 'im."

"I'll go along with Fearless Leader here. You keep going down. Hopefully it's low enough that he's okay again. Same path we went. No detours. We're hitting the crater then coming right back."

Nilesh stared at each of us, as Cy stared at the ground. "Okay."

I could tell Cy wanted to chime in but I didn't let him.

"You're not going alone. We've had enough clusterfucks for one day."

❧

His limp was more pronounced. I let him lead the way to the crater. We rounded more and more to the right, from patch of rocky ground to patch of rocky ground. Little bits of ice started to crystallize on the slabs—I was careful not to slip on these. It was freezing, and my generic rain poncho did little to help at that level. Each chilling gust increased the already hard bumps on my skin. My teeth clattered as I hugged myself deep at the armpits.

"Cy . . . Where ya going?"

"I'm going to walk 'round the top."

I clenched my teeth to steady my jaw. "Just be careful, man. I-I can barely move an inch already . . ."

"The wind's pushing over the hill. The worst of it. You sure you won't come with?"

"Nah, man. No . . . I'm done. I'm here in case something goes wrong, but I can't do any more." Another drip, drip from my nose. "Hurry. We've got Yūhi to think about."

"Okay." He pointed with his chin, the skin on his face glowing with orange. "Look, it's starting."

I glanced back and saw it in one breathtaking sweep: the sun piercing from just beyond the horizon, dripping with it a wave of heat and a wide splash of neon that trickled, distorting all colors in the sky. I could feel the warmth on my skin, but still lost in the cold air. It was kind of an interesting feeling. Freezing cold yet this beautiful warmth.

I continued to stare as Cy limped away. It was mesmerizing. I had never seen any sunrise like that before, ever, and never again would. So incredible. Like, it wasn't just the land or the sky or the cosmos and environment but rather, time itself. I was witnessing the future and the past simultaneously, perhaps everything in between.

Baby . . .

Twirling the promise ring on my finger, I continued to stare into the rising sun. I didn't blink but instead kept my eyes half-squinted. I thought about taking out my composition book (now with no cover) and sketching, but I just couldn't turn away.

Something was happening. Then, there. Inside me. Within the world.

One of the most spectacular things I ever witnessed, hands down. I just took it in. All of it. The forests, the lake. The long slope going down the side. The layer of cloud floating beneath us and swirling counterclockwise. The sun unraveling, first as a small crescent, then already growing into a bright half-circle. How much time had passed since I stopped and stared, I could not know. In fact, maybe it stood still altogether.

10

Neither of us said a thing for a while on the way back down to the others. Our eyes continually gazed at our feet then up at the sun, then down again. After we rounded a sharp bend with a big rock jutting out, we saw Nilesh and Yūhi resting on the ground. One of them waved and we both waved back. Cy reached into his rucksack.

"Hey, remember my cam'ra?" He pulled out the device, now cracked at multiple places.

"Oh. Crap."

"Yeah. Must be from when I took that drop."

I glanced down, shook my head, hands in my pockets. He was gazing up at the sky again.

"Ah. Nothing beats seeing it with your bare eyes, anyways."

Wiping at my forehead, I nodded along.

"Listen. I've got an idea." He took the map from his back pocket, started to unfold it.

"What?"

"If we crossed, say, here . . ." He pointed, showing me. "We could maybe cut our time by half."

"That such a good idea? I mean, what if we get lost?"

In the distance, I could see Nilesh put on a hat then hand

over his handkerchief. It appeared like Yūhi was wiping blood from his nose.

"He's quite in bad shape, really. The sooner we get down, the better."

Staring at the map close, I could see where the path forked off.

Hmm. Spider-sense tingling . . .

"All right, then. Let's try."

❧

Walking down was even more difficult than walking up. My legs were flimsy and already trembling. Each slow step sank into a deep layer of crumbled gravel. There were rocks stuck in my shoes and socks, and the soles were coming apart. My face was caked in dirt.

This side of the mountain was different. While the other side was solid with some rocks, this one was all piles of rocks. Layers and layers of broken rock.

"I don't see why we couldn't go back the way we came . . ." I heard Nilesh cry out, frustrated. "This terrain, it's unforgiving."

"It's 'cause the way we came would be too steep."

"This takes us back to the original path, just less of an angle. Right, Cy?"

". . . Yes." He was getting tired from all the limping, I could tell. "A little quicker, and safer. Trust me."

We were all growing tired of this slippery new gravel. Each rock would roll under our feet. If it wasn't a slip over gravel or a literal rolling stone, then it was sinking down in a whole layer of it. It was pure agony. Tired from each step alone, amplified by having to also pull our foot out from being buried. The rocks destroyed my skater shoes and tore the bottoms of my baggy jeans. I had pebbles in my pockets. To this day, I still find pebbles in that hoodie. Whenever I see it hanging in the closet, I can taste the pebbles.

The sun beamed down and heated up the ground. It started burning with each step. Now it was real bright, and became difficult to see. We each put sunglasses on, except Nilesh who wore a hat. A trickle of sweat dripped from my forehead down to my cheek then my neck. Between heat waves, strong gusts spun around, sending tiny red particles up in the air that we struggled to keep out of our eyes.

Nilesh held a palm to his forehead, splashed water on his face. Yūhi crossed his arms over his abdomen. Cy began hopping to keep the weight off his swollen ankle.

I felt a light tap on my arm.

". . . Here."

"What?"

"I can't. You gotta take over. You remember, right? The cut to the Gotemba path."

I stopped, held onto the map. I immediately wanted to give it back but somehow couldn't. "And we're on track?"

"Should be. Or we'd have to backtrack that whole way."

We both stared up the steep incline.

"Oh, God, no . . ."

I don't wanna end up some poor soul on the slopes on the news. I just want to go home. I have to. Please.

I could see Yūhi gag a little. Nilesh was breathing hard. It seemed like Cy's ankle bruised up to the shin already, the wrapping seeping through with blood. I folded the map, put it away in my back pocket, and took the lead. It was me in front, Nilesh, then Yūhi, then Cy.

11

THE DAY BEFORE, when we first arrived, it was later in the afternoon. It took us several hours to make it up to the cabin. We rested there a couple hours, then arrived at the top in another few hours. And there we all were, still at it, how many hours later. It had been at least a good twenty hours all together. Twenty hours of struggles and setbacks and torture.

I sipped water and rechecked the map for the thousandth time. Everyone was dead silent. Nobody took any breaks. Nobody had any new suggestions or ideas. No music blasted from the mini-speaker. We all just wanted to get the hell off that damn mountain.

I hoped then that I led the guys the right way. 'Cause if not, that would be another five hours, easy. Backtrack, then course correct, and hopefully get it right.

Our bodies were ragdolls by then. More than that, our minds were wrung through and turned into paste. We had nothing left.

It was taking a lot longer than I expected . . .

A slight panic set in.

The one thing that helped keep me going was mental displacement. My mind was with my girl back home: her eyes, her lips, her body. I thought about the park by my house. The pond, the pads. Cicadas in the distance so beautiful, so annoying. I thought about the crane perched on the small bridge.

Up ahead, I noticed the path gradually bend in the opposite direction.

Oh. Shit, wait. Is this the wrong *way?*

I held the crinkled map tight as gusts whipped, frantically darted left then right.

W-which way? Which way!?

I stopped, lowered the map, felt my bottom lip begin to quiver . . . I had gotten us turned around after all. I shut my eyelids, hard. How in the hell was I going to tell them.

My head hung down, I could feel the sun on the back of my neck as I clenched my fists, either to keep from crying or to keep from screaming. Or both. I had reached my breaking point.

They each walked past me one by one, clapped me on the shoulder, playfully smacked and pinched my cheek.

"Well done, mate. Well done."

I could feel Cy limp past. I could hear Nilesh and Yūhi laugh and cheer. I opened my eyes again, couldn't believe what I was seeing. It didn't make any sense.

On the other side of the bend was the Gotemba path. By some wild miracle or stroke of sheer luck, we had made it down.

All these years later, and I still think about it. The mountain. The top of the mountain, the crater. The sunrise. Only a fool climbs Mount Akaiwa twice—I get that now. From the elements to the terrain, to bad luck. Hurt ankles and broken cameras, to almost passing out, to throwing up and difficulty breathing. I had almost given up in the beginning, many times, but I'm so glad I kept going, foolish though it was.

INBOUND

1

Many things can happen in a thirty-eight hour span. A woman can give birth. A boy could catch a cold or a flu. A man can almost drive across the country, coast to coast. Someone's whole entire life could change. In thirty-eight hours, the world could turn upside down. Life can flip on a dime and send a person off in a different direction. It could be thirty-eight hours of joy, it could be thirty-eight hours of pain and torture. For the hundreds of thousands of unsuspecting citizens across a specific tristate area, sheer terror would soon sweep through. Terror that would be impossible to undo or redirect and would have disastrous results.

The leash pulled taut, the loop almost slipping from his hand. It wasn't clear who was dragging who, who was trying to hold the other back. A tug-of-war had ensued since the moment he opened the car door, from the asphalt parking lot to the concrete walking path, along the hills lining the stream. She went from the base of one palm tree to the other, to bushes, to various plants of the community garden. Scratch and sniff and dig and paw, repeat. This wasn't quite how he expected his weekend to begin, yet with no one around to take care of the little runt, he was stuck on dog sitting duty. He was a little kid when he last had a dog himself, but his neighbor was desperate. It would just be two and a half days, that's all. What's the worst that could happen? Famous last words, as it were.

"Hey. Mari, c'mon. Let up."

They called her Mari for short. Her full name was Mariana. Mariana Pickle, to be exact. She was a young, spunky Jack Russell terrier Schnauzer mix, tri-colored black, white and goldish brown. A beautiful and brilliant creature, but also a current pain in his ass.

"Gimme a break, will ya . . ."

If it were his usual solo walk, it was very peaceful in this area. There would be families having picnics, children playing in the sandbox, couples lying together watching the clouds in the sky, a team of paddlers gathering equipment, an old lady feeding the ducks. Or maybe those were all there, but he didn't have a chance to notice as he had the leash in one hand, tugging him left then right then straight, and plastic bags in the other.

He noticed all of a sudden that it indeed was peaceful out, but perhaps too peaceful. It was quiet, empty, like something might be off. For an early Saturday morning, there should have been a decent amount of people riding their bicycles, practicing their free throw, jogging, doing pull-ups.

That's weird.

Hmm.

Across the way, on the other side of the stream where there were benches lined, he saw some people running. Not running for sport, but running as if they were late for an appointment or something important had come up.

Behind that, a couple cars sped past, seeming out of place.

He furled his brow, shrugged, made his way back to the

parking lot. He could hear the dog panting and the sound of her paws on the pavement.

As he grabbed the keys from his pocket, there was someone else nearby fumbling for their own keys, in a hurried walk, with a worried look. Sitting under the gazebo, somebody else wept, and appeared to be praying, begging.

"Mari. Get in the car, girl."

It was an old (and bad) habit to not bring his phone whenever he went for a walk. These walks would last about an hour or so but today just a half an hour, since he had to go to work still. Usual work days for him were Monday through Friday but his student asked to switch a day this week.

His job was to work with children with disabilities on various skillsets. It could be social skills, it could be handwriting or counting money. Sometimes it was a community task like going to the store, crossing the street or taking the bus.

This particular child he had grown close to, always happy to see him.

As the dog hopped from the floor to the seat to in his lap behind the steering wheel, as if she were the real driver, he reached for his phone.

BALLISTIC MISSILE THREAT INBOUND.
SEEK IMMEDIATE SHELTER.
THIS IS NOT A DRILL.

Everything all at once fell away, faded and sank. The phone was about to slip from his hand as he stared, vacant, shocked, in disbelief.

"T-t-that can't be. What the—"

Without thinking, he tried to call his family but to no avail. It rang a couple times then cut out. He tried calling his friends, but it wouldn't go through. He even tried calling 9-1-1. Nothing.

In the corner of the screen, there were zero bars. No calls, no text. No data.

How can this be happening?

Before his walk, he still had reception. The notification must have been during the time he and the dog took their stroll. Not sure what happened then. Maybe the response overwhelmed the system, overloaded the cellular network towers.

Turning the key, he started the car, saw the gauge rise a notch above E. As he swallowed a lump of dry air, he wondered where to go, what to do.

Ah, shit. Wait. Wait a freaking sec.

I can't just leave him . . .

What if he's waiting there? All by himself!?

"Hold on, girl. We gotta drive a li'l fast here." The seatbelt clicked then he rubbed his fingertips over her tiny head between her ears. "Just gonna check on the kid, make sure he's okay. Okay?"

She stuck her tongue out, tilted her nose up at him, oblivious, blissful and unaware.

2

As he drove through the city streets, it was more of the same worried looks, people crying, people running, getting in their cars and speeding off. A truck raced past in the other direction, the force from it shaking the entire car like a sudden gust. Still unsure how he felt about this whole thing, he mulled it over in his mind, tried to make sense of it. Could this be a hoax? Could this be a terrible mistake? Did some overpaid idiot push the button by accident? Or was this real? In the end, he concluded it wasn't worth taking that chance. Either way, it didn't matter right now. If the kid was alone and afraid and in danger, how could he live with himself, with whatever little time there was left or not left.

Holy God . . .

There, before his eyes, was one of the strangest and saddest things. Pressing on the brake to gawk, to rubberneck, his eyes narrowed as he watched the scene unfolding before him. A concerned father removed a manhole cover then lowered his confused children into the storm drain one at a time.

"It has officially gone from nuts to apeshit."

He pushed the gas pedal, hard, speeding back up, taking a long left turn over the freeway on-ramp.

Mariana repositioned down on her haunches, lowering her ears with a slight whimper.

"I know, I know. Sorry but we gotta go."

From the freeway, he could see the college campus and hordes of students running between buildings across the lawns. Maybe they were told to seek shelter, to find cover. Maybe they had designated basement areas, or something.

As he drove, it was like a race to the finish line. He was already going seventy-five in a sixty, and still, cars were overtaking him.

Come on, come on, come on.

Come the fuck on!

Sirens blared and cut through the air then, loud and sharp.

Every first of the month was a routine test of the emergency broadcast system. It was common to have thunderstorms and flash floods, sometimes threat of a possible tsunami so these were so often unalarming. This time, however, was different. It sounded different. It felt different. Like an omen. An uneasy dread set in.

It transitioned from the freeway to a highway. The light turned yellow but he made it in time, took the second left, the suspension bouncing as they entered the side street. There was a family packing boxes into the back of their SUV. Another family boarded up their windows with plywood.

Just like he feared, there the kid was, standing on the corner waiting with his baseball cap on, backpack tight around his shoulders, with a happy-go-lucky smile. The notification arrived just before their appointment, and there was no way his parents could have foreseen this. As the child ran over and waved, he rolled the window down. The sirens were even louder with the window open.

"Mister Charles! Mister Charles!"

The way he spoke, with a slight lisp, always sounded like he said "mitter." It was endearing, and grew to have a certain senti-mental value.

"You okay? Is your phone working?"

"Nope. I gots the alert then it die. I can't even play Pokémon Go."

His pronounced lisp also made his Ls and Rs sound a lot like Ws. Kind of cute.

"Ah, geez. Get in. Get in." He shook his head then motioned with his hand. "We better go."

"Hey. You brought a dog?"

"Kind of. Her name's Mari."

The kid turned his palm over and Mariana leaned over and licked it.

"Good doggy."

"Which way's your house? Are your parents home?"

"My house just down the road." The kid reached with both hands and rubbed under Mariana's neck. "But they not home."

"You're kidding . . ."

"On the weekend, me, my mommy and my daddy go visit grandma. I didn't go today 'cause our training."

Ah, shit.

"And where does your grandmother live?"

The kid smiled wide, way too upbeat despite the circum-stances. With a missile incoming, communications disrupted, sirens blaring in the distance, all he noticed was the fuzzy animal.

"She has a big, big house out in Kwalhioqua."

"That's like the other side of . . ."

Just then, the LOW FUEL warning light ticked on.

"Dang it. Perfect."

"Are we driving out there, Mister Charles?"

"I told you, Tyler. You don't have to say 'Mister.' Just Charles." He spun the wheel, spun the car around. "And yes."

3

In the last few months, there had been a heightened level of tension between countries, with missile test launches provoking the boundaries between territories. Global concerns about the risk of nuclear weapons being used between the US and its perceived enemies was growing, and of retaliation from other countries like a domino effect. A new brazen and unconventional president mocked world leaders with silly nicknames and taunted them over the size of their button. Take your pick of potential threats—from Russia to China to North Korea—the alert made absolute sense. Many comparisons were drawn to the state of the Cold War. It pretty much dominated all the headlines.

"This is crazy, huh, Mister Charles. It's like *War of the Worlds* out there, or maybe *The Walking Dead.*"

Charles didn't respond, kept his eye on the road.

He passed the first gas station by mistake. Not as familiar with the area, and not all there in mind and body, Charles functioned in panic mode but also struggled to appear calm. The second gas station was packed full from every side, overflowing with cars blocking each other in and honking. Drivers rolled their window down, waved balled fists and cursed.

The needle hovered over E. The LOW FUEL light continued to shine on.

Can't keep pushing it . . .

"W-where's the nearest gas station, Tyler? Do you know?"

"Yeah. Take the next right."

"Next light? Next right?" Again, it was hard to tell his Ls and his Rs.

"Over there!"

His hands jerked the wheel as the child pointed over the dashboard. Mariana slid on his lap but dug her claws and withstood the sharp turn.

The third gas station was empty except for a handful of people. A dingy facility, in an isolated location, but it would have to do.

Last two spots were open. He took the one closest to the store.

"Stay in the car, Ty." Charles stepped out, panned from left to right.

In the far front was an old man who left his key in the ignition and ran inside. There was a couple rotating the gas cap back on, about to leave. A middle-aged woman had just pulled up.

"Mari, be good."

Two sketchy types talked amongst themselves, nudging their elbows and pointing with their chins. One had dark sunglasses, and one had a baggy jacket. He kept a close eye on them.

Mind your business, assholes.

He swiped his card but it didn't go through. He swiped again.

"Are you kidding me? Tyler, I gotta go in, pay cash. Guess

the internet's down, like the phones. You wait here. And be careful."

"Got it." The child was busy playing with the dog.

As he walked in, the old man finished up and exited. He went to the counter, opened his wallet then heard yelling outside. His head darted over and he peeked through the window. It wasn't his car. It wasn't the lady.

The old man yelled, Hey! Hey! Hey!!! Though the man tried to chase them, it was way too late, as the hoodlums hopped off the curb and disappeared down the street. With the loud screeching, the faint smell of burnt rubber filled the air. The man continued that direction in a defeated stance, kicking himself, hanging his head low.

Poor guy . . .

"Hey, Ty! Everything okay?" He leaned in the passenger window.

"Yup. That old man, though. They tooks his car."

"I saw." Charles went around to the driver's side, started to pump. "Things are falling apart. We gotta get you to your parents, A-S-A-P."

"What about him?"

"Tyler, we don't know him. We can't trust that person."

He finished pumping, watching the old man still, then got inside.

As he reversed, then turned the other way back onto the main road, he could see the old man in his rearview mirror still. He walked with a slight hunch, a cane in hand.

Tyler glanced over his shoulder out the back window, jutting out his lower lip. It seemed like Mariana did as well.

"God damn it. Okay, okay. Fine. We will ask if he needs a ride, but that's it. This ain't a taxi service."

They pulled a U-turn and approached nice and slow, as

to not alarm him. Up close, the man wore a plaid shirt and khakis, had thick glasses on.

"Hey, um . . ." Charles swallowed, speaking over Tyler to the sidewalk. "We're headed toward Kwalhioqua, if you need a ride, mister."

Without a word, the old man shifted, with sunken eyes and his mouth open. After a slight pause, he nodded then got in back.

"Nooo!" Tyler yelled out. "Pokémon still don't work!"

Charles shook his head, smirked. "This is Tyler. The dog's Mariana. My name is Charles. You?"

". . . Serj."

It reminded him of his favorite soda as a kid, that had since been discontinued.

4

THE NEXT GAS station that they passed had an impromptu sign posted out front: ALL SOLD OUT. Charles tightened his grip on the wheel and grinded his teeth, then scanned his surroundings. More cars sped past in the other direction, honking as they did. Some groups walked on foot now, almost celebrating, cheering, hooting, welcoming whatever it was to come. Mariana closed her eyes and snoozed. Tyler took his cap off, brushed his fingers through his hair, then put his cap back on. He then adjusted the dials, trying to tune in to anything to help kill the time and fill in the silence. He tapped at the plastic piece in frustration.

"The radio don't work, Mister Charles."

"Not surprised." Charles gazed in the rearview. "Serj, know anything at all, 'bout what's going on?"

At first, the old man continued to stare. Out the window, the sirens blaring blended with the sound of a firetruck in the distance. While he tweedled his thumbs in his lap, it seemed Serj contemplated his next words.

"It could happen any minute now."

What?

His eyes shifted in the mirror, locked with the old man.

"Been too long already as is. I remember a news program once, saying that it would take somewhere between twelve and fifteen minutes for an intercontinental ballistic missile to hit here. Twenty minutes tops, depending where it was coming from."

"So, what you think we should do?"

"In the fifties, we had civil defense drills. They were all the same." Serj returned to dazing out the window while he spoke. "Got to get inside, go underground."

"Under . . . ground?"

"Yes, like the basement of a big building, in the center of it. Far from the roof as possible, from all the exterior walls. When that bomb hits, more than just the blast, it'll be nuclear fallout coming down. Intensely radioactive." The man shook his head. "Have to get a half a mile from the explosion, at least twenty to thirty feet inside somewhere. It could save your life."

Charles licked his lips as he furled his brow. He glanced over to the passenger seat where Tyler continued to tweak at the dials and buttons. Mariana nuzzled against his torso, still asleep.

"If it takes twelve to fifteen for the bomb to hit, how long before we would need to get inside?

"Well, it would be best if you already were in shelter. But, I suppose it could be another fifteen to twenty minutes if you could avoid the fallout. And the shockwave from the explosion, of course. Then it would be survival."

Hmm . . .

"You might need to stay in place for twenty-four to forty-eight hours, minimum. It could be six hours. It could be two to three days, or two weeks. Hell, maybe even two years if the world fires back at one another like god damned maniacs. This could be it, for all we know."

"Jesus Christ." Charles faced down then faced back up. "So, I mean, what should we do then?"

"Stop for supplies, then hide somewhere, plain and simple. Maybe someone you know has a wine cellar?"

He shook his head, in response but also in disbelief.

"You would need jugs of water, energy bars, canned goods—"

Tyler chimed in. "Don't forget a can opener!"

"—flashlight and batteries. A hand crank radio, TV maybe, for when the airwaves ever go back up."

"Any other ideas?"

"I mean, I've heard that Pearlmount has a network of concrete tunnels beneath it, like a labyrinth. To keep the government running. For key officials to operate in a crisis. I know there was an artillery barrage there during the war. Would have been designed to withstand attacks, to hold equipment and materials, continue chain of command, keep comms running, like a hub."

His eyes narrowed. "Is that Pearlmount or Pearlcrest?"

"Pearlmount. Pearlmount Summit."

Charles slapped the steering wheel. "God. That's all the way back where I started. We're far from both now, of course. Shit."

Tyler giggled. "Mister Charles, you said 'shit' . . ."

"Yeah, yeah."

"Hey, you just said 'shit' too, young man." Serj smiled to himself.

Tyler giggled again, which turned to a chortle and a squeal.

As they drove through the long mountain tunnel, there were cars pulled over to the side of the road by the walls. They passed these with caution. Some people hugged each other. Others held hands. More weeping, more praying. Less running.

5

IN THE CROWDED parking lot of the superstore, madness began to flare. There were people running in and out, bags in each hand, bags full. Some of them shoved at one another, forcing their way through. Some of them walked slow, as a precaution, with their guard up. One person tripped, fell, landed on their face. Charles parked in a faraway stall in the back, driving along slow. Serj stepped out, watched the scene occurring before them in silence. It was as if these people had become rabid animals in a frenzy, or madmen in an asylum during the full moon. Normal upstanding citizens descended into savagery.

"This could get ugly . . ."

"I know." Charles also stood, kept the door open, leaned in. "Tyler, you wanna wait or come in?"

"I'm scared, Mister Charles."

"You better stay close, I think. Mari?"

The doggy raised its head with a loud and sharp bark, right on cue.

It was the old man, cane in hand, the kid with a limp, himself, then the little dog. All four walked towards the entrance.

Mariana let out a subdued growl, yanking Charles ahead in small spurts, causing him to feel like a freak on a leash.

As they neared the doors, someone ran out with a big box in their hands. It might have been a TV set but he wasn't sure, didn't get a good enough look. Another person ran out carrying a pile of smaller boxes, maybe smartphones or tablets.

Did he pay for that?

"This is absolute pandemonium." Serj now had a glare on his face, as they went in, saw everything up close. "Insanity."

People loaded up their carts and their baskets in a hurry. The shelves were almost empty, with just a few items left.

"Grab that toilet paper, Ty."

"Be careful, young man."

It was the very last one. The kid hobbled over, grabbed it, holding it close to his body as he limped back, like a quarter-back making a first down.

"We'll need flashlights, batteries."

"Leave it to me." Serj went down one of the aisles.

"Start grabbing food. Canned, in a package. It's gotta be non-perishable."

". . . Non-perishable?"

"Like, has to be able to last a long, long time."

"Ah, gotcha." Tyler limped away.

"Hey. Just take what we need to survive. Right?"

The kid nodded with a big smile.

Serj came back with a basket. "What's with the child, anyway? Down syndrome?"

"I'm not supposed to say but . . . Lot of his peers have that, sure. Autism too. But he has cerebral palsy, plus mild brain injury. He was one of the top players in his special league 'til he took one right here." Charles pointed to the side of his head. "His upper body is still great, nice and strong, but his processing was affected. That, with the limp in his right leg already . . ."

"He's a good boy."

Charles moved the leash from one hand to the other as Mariana circled around him, assessing the situation. "Just gotta get him back to his fam."

The old man thinned his lips. "Again, it could happen any moment now."

Tyler returned with a couple canned goods, a few packs of noodles, started loading them into the basket. "That's all they had."

"I said, just take what we need to survive."

"What? These are fidgets—"

"Folks, folks." The worker with a pink vest on and big button pin held their hands up as they spoke. "We will be closing our registers in ten minutes. We aren't taking cards at the moment, it has to be cash payment."

The crowd groaned and shouted in frustration.

"Our manager wants everyone to evacuate this area. It is a matter of safety here, sir." The worker shook their head, slinked backward as the uproar intensified. "Folks, folks. Folks!"

Alarms began to ring out across the store. Half the fluorescent lights above turned off. There was the sound of glass shattering, items toppling down, then cries of mixed rage and panic.

Ducking low, motioning with his hand, Charles led them through the store. Mariana pulled in front, quick, leading him in turn.

"Get that water and let's go!"

Whatever last semblance of order crumbled. People smashed open glass display cases, snatched whatever they could, whatever they wanted. People wrestled over who got the last bottle of medicine, the last box of panty liners, the last pack of blankets—the last baby formula. They loaded up their carts high like a shopping spree. Rubbish cans were knocked over and scattered on the floor. Greed and opportunism at its very worst.

Lines to the register turned to lines racing out the automatic doors. Charles and Mariana jogged to the front, Serj right behind, then Tyler.

"We're not paying?"

"Fuck it. We gotta go."

Serj shook his head, following along at first, but turned around as his conscience kicked in. He took out his wallet and dropped three twenties on the counter. The cashier shrugged, overwhelmed, unsure where to even begin. The bag boy threw off his vest and ran out with the crowd.

Mariana stood watch, growling and barking as the chaos ensued. Charles and Tyler loaded the toilet paper, batteries, flashlights, packs of noodles, canned goods and bottles of water all in the trunk. Serj caught up, took the basket and went to the far return area to put it away with the carts. With everything going on, the old man still had a conscience, still had respect and morals and dignity.

As they were about to get in the car, a lady nearby let out a sharp shriek. She was surrounded by hooligans trying to grab at her purse. There were about four or five of them, wearing leather gloves and denim clothes.

"Oh, shit."

"What do we do, Mister Charles?"

Charles turned to Serj but he was gone, went over and knocked one of the punks right in the head with his cane.

If it were a regular cane with a single point, it already would have hurt, but this was the kind with four prongs on the bottom and one of the prongs was missing a rubber tip.

"Ow!!! You crazy-ass old FUCK!"

Serj then went and choked the other from behind with the quad cane turned sideways, hopping on the guy's back.

Before another one got too close, Tyler threw a fidget spinner right at his face, hitting his eye and the bridge of his nose at the same time.

"What the—"

Charles hit the bastard in his jaw with a straight cross, kicked him in his rib, away from the woman. Next to her now, he could tell she was pregnant. She held a palm over her stomach, held the other hand up in defense. A bigger guy started running toward Charles but Mariana clamped down on his pants leg, ripping the cloth by his knee and shin, forcing him to slip and stumble.

The lady stood behind Charles who clenched both fists in an attack stance. Mariana bared her fangs, barked. Tyler held another spinner in his right hand, at the ready. Serj waved the cane over his head like a wild baboon.

"You know what, bitch?" The punk signaled his punk friends. "Now no one can have it."

One doused the SUV in gasoline, while the other lit a match.

Glug, glug, glug.

Sizzle.

No, no, no, no!

The fireball mushroomed in dark orange, with thick black fumes rising up, forcing them all backward.

Like a pack of hyenas, the hooligans ran off laughing and snickering. A working vehicle destroyed, fuel wasted, but the worst part—the woman's reaction. Her brows furled, her lids fell, mouth scrunched as she covered her face with both hands, breaking down and sniffling.

"Here, Ty." Charles handed the leash. "Take Mari back to the car. You wanna ride with us, miss?"

She continued to sob into her palms, shuddering throughout her upper body. He patted her on the shoulder, motioned with his hand to follow, to join them. At last, she nodded back, wiping away the streams of tears.

"Okay, let's go . . ."

Before Tyler and Mariana could open the car door, with Charles and the pregnant lady following close behind, Serj dropped his quad cane and fell to one knee.

Each turned around. He clutched a hand over his chest, gritted his teeth between groans, as he slumped forward and down.

"Serj!!!"

6

Pulling through the city streets, it was a different world. Store windows were bashed open. Looters hopped in and out, loaded their vans and trucks then hopped right back in. It was like a busy line of fire ants devouring their dying prey, ripping apart their insides bit by bit for their fattened queen. Rioters hurled bricks, busted car windows, headlights and tail lights, and banged on hoods and fenders with crowbars and sledgehammers, whatever other blunt objects they could get their hands on. A few garbage cans and dumpsters were ablaze, crackling away in a bright wavering flurry. A police car and a city bus burned side by side. There was the vague sound of a firetruck in the distance, but it seemed in vain. Fires outnumbered the firetrucks at an exponential rate.

The ride from the superstore was a blur, other than some random person hurling a liquor bottle that startled them and cracked the driver's side window. Tyler pet Mariana, staring out the window, gazing at the anarchy. Serj lay in the back seat, perspiring, struggling to breathe, unable to speak. The pregnant woman comforted him. Charles pressed the pedal with the ball of his foot, yanked the wheel left, right, avoiding flying debris and various rubbish littering the road, trying to remain calm despite the circumstances.

"Mister Charles, is he gonna be okay?"

"I hope so, Tyler."

He watched as the dog licked away at the child's palm. She then nibbled and chewed her treat in his lap.

"My name is Charles. This is Tyler, Mariana. That's Serj. What's your name?"

The woman returned a vacant expression.

"Do you speak . . . English?"

She shook her head, faced down.

"I'm Charles." He pointed to his chest then to her, in the mirror. "And you?"

"Y-Yanlin."

"Yanlin? Yanlin." He nodded to himself in affirmation. "Yanlin, do you have anybody waiting for you? Anywhere you need to be?"

She shook her head.

"We're going to the hospital now. If you need, you can stay with us. No problem. But maybe they have a better phone system there. I don't know. If there's anyone you need to get in contact with . . ."

He pulled into the emergency area, stopped in the front of the wide roundabout. From the side of the building, an ambulance rushed out, lights flashing. Other cars waited ahead of them, the occupants explaining, pleading with some of the staff.

Charles leaned out of the window. "Somebody! Help!"

An attendant took notice, glanced their way.

"This man, he's had a heart attack!!! Please!"

Raising a finger, the attendant turned and hurried over with a walkie-talkie, peeped in the back seat.

Personnel raced out, preparing a stretcher.

"ER is overflowing. But we can bypass the others in a life-or-death situation. Move your car then go to the waiting area. When he's stable, you can go up to the room. Not many beds left. Good timing."

7

It was cramped in the hospital room. However, compared to hours in the waiting room, a major improvement. Tyler and Mariana played together at first but both fell asleep, taking a much needed nap. Yanlin didn't say anything, just rubbed her stomach, staring down at her feet. Charles paced back and forth, wondering, worrying, not just about the present moment but the not-too-distant future. Now he went from pacing to sitting, as the others stretched their legs. There was a chair by the window, where he could see plumes of smoke still rising in parts of the city. Helicopters roamed in the darkening skies. The sirens had since stopped. From dawn, this started to spiral out of control and will have lasted, soon, until dusk.

Just as Charles felt compelled to stay with Tyler, all felt compelled to stay with Serj, though each had their own families, their own priorities. With their fate still unclear, the hospital was as good a place as any to hide out or stay put. Plus, the matter was settled once the chaos resulted in fallen telephone poles which blocked the streets. They moved the food, water and supplies inside with them.

Others in the waiting room asked some of the staff about the phones, about the internet. Still no concrete answer. It did seem, though, that enough time had passed that the missile threat may have waned. No one could be certain. There was still the possibility until their governor, their mayor, their congresswoman—someone in authority—said otherwise. For now, another crisis was at hand, the panic having turned volatile and unruly, resulting in roaming mobs in the streets.

Bang.

Bang, bang.

He peered into the distant cityscape, wondering what the sound could be. Was it the police with shields and batons, with gas canisters? Was it the army? Was it the reserves, the national guard? Or maybe it was propane tanks caught in the fires spreading. Maybe it was tires popping. Maybe it was all in his imagination.

The nurse stepped in, clipboard in hand.

"No new updates as of now. As I already told you, he suffered a myocardial infarction. A heart attack. But he is stable, for the moment. At least he's off the ventilator and breathing on his own, though a bit labored."

Charles sat up, listened.

Tyler leaned on the armrest. Mariana sprawled across his tennis shoes.

Yanlin turned to the hospital bed with a somber look.

Serj lay there, his chest rising and falling, a disturbed expression on his face like he might be uncomfortable. As the machine bleeped, displaying numbers and graphs, oxygen pumped from the hose in the wall through the nasal cannula.

"If you noticed, the lights flickered a little while ago. We are running on generator power. There is rumor of rolling blackouts, from the fires."

The nurse let them have a moment. Yanlin didn't understand but knew it was serious. Tyler and Mariana were quiet, patient. Charles rubbed his fingers across his brow, the lids of his eyes, then down his lips to his chin.

"And what does that mean . . . ?"

"Our generators are tested every few months, so they're working. Depending how much fuel was used during the last test, this place can run between forty-eight to ninety-six hours."

Charles could sense a "but."

"But . . ."

Aha.

"Something in the transition did mess with our oxygen system. Whatever's in the tanks, in the tubes, that is it until further notice. Maintenance is working hard to get everything going again. Please let us know if you see signs of respiratory distress."

"What happens if he does show 'respiratory distress' . . . Then what? Is he going to be okay?"

"I mean, we have spare tanks, extra concentrators, yes. But I do wanna be honest with you." There was trepidation in her voice as she crossed her arms, holding the clipboard over her chest. "Our building is at max capacity. We have a lot of people. And more are coming in every minute, every hour. I don't know what might happen."

The nurse waved, bowed, turned to leave.

God damn. Could this get any worse?

"Oh. And it does seem that some people, depending on your carrier, are getting service back, internet back. I can't say for sure but it sounds like the missile threat has passed."

Charles took a breath in and out.

"So at least that's one less thing. If we could just fix what's going on in here, and what's going on out there . . ." She pointed with her chin out the window. "Well, we might just have a chance. Anyway. If you need anything, lemme know. I'll be back to check on you guys."

Yanlin tapped Charles on the shoulder, raised her brows and shrugged.

He pointed to the light. "The power is out. They're on generators."

She furled her brow.

He pointed to the tube of oxygen. "The air is limited. Their system shut off."

She held a hand to her mouth then stepped aside.

"Mister Charles?"

"Yeah, Ty."

"If there is so many people and only a little oxygen, could he die? Could other people die too?"

Charles didn't respond, instead watched as Yanlin rummaged through the drawers.

"Everybody, stop breathing!" Tyler inhaled deep then pinched his nose.

Yanlin was scribbling with paper and pen, bent over the table. Charles stood and joined her.

"What is this?"

Tyler shut his eyes, shuddered, struggling to hold his breath. His cheeks began to turn red.

She tapped the drawing, pointed to an X.

"A, uh . . . A map?

Yanlin nodded, motioned with two fingers like footsteps.

"I can walk?"

Yanlin nodded again while Tyler let out his breath and gasped.

"Hmm. I don't know."

Just then, Serj coughed and wheezed. The machines dinged and alarmed before normalizing again.

"Ah, crap."

"I'll go with you, Mister Charles!"

"No. No, Tyler." Charles knocked the tabletop with a closed fist, sighed.

Tyler stepped forward. "But it might dangerous by yourself."

"You're right. You're right." Charles touched the top of the boy's cap. "And that's why you need to stay here with these guys. Okay? Hold down the fort."

Mariana whimpered from the floor. Yanlin placed her hands on her hips, sat on the edge of the bed. Serj tossed then turned. Charles stood to leave.

"I'll go it alone from here."

8

From the hospital, it was a straight shot for a good few blocks. Then it would be a zigzag, left-right, left-left-right, to the pharmacy. It was night now, and all the nocturnal creatures had awakened. They were hungry. They were thirsty. They were crazed. As he walked further into the city, Charles covered his mouth with the collar of his shirt. The streets were hazy with smoke from the fires burning. In some parts, enough cars and dumpsters were lit that it was bright like an afternoon sunset. In others, the streetlights were dim, and it was difficult to see his own footing. On the corner ahead by the intersection, Charles saw a group hurling bricks at an electronics store. The glass cracked but somehow remained intact. Must have been reinforced.

The stores past it, one with flowers, one with lighting fixtures, one with fireworks, had been raided. Had things been different, he would be buying flowers for his date or playing with sparklers and cherry bombs.

When the group tried the next one, a jewelry store, the front windows shattered and fell like grains of sugar.

Charles watched them swarm in and out, like piranhas, like wasps. He moved to the far sidewalk to keep his distance.

Jesus . . .

It was a far cry from when the public ran for cover and rushed to get underground. A different people. A different place. Sirens in the distance were replaced now by car alarms and alarms from security systems.

Behind him, he heard a woman scream. Unlike the parking lot of the superstore, he was all alone, and felt powerless. He turned, walked, then turned again, the first left-right.

A car sped past then screeched to a halt. There was the violent sound of metal banging, yelling, shouting. The car was surrounded by a vicious crowd that kicked the fenders, jumped up and down on the hood and roof, ripped open the doors and dragged the occupants out.

Oh, God . . .

That is why he chose to walk versus drive.

He continued to the next set of turns, the left-left-right. Police cars drove through, slow, flashing intermittent red and blue, aiming their flashlights into alleyways. Charles jogged away from them.

Ducking low, he strafed the brick wall of an empty bar. Across the street, there was graffiti sprawled over the pillars of a national bank. Up ahead, at last, Charles spotted the big vertical sign with kanji letters.

I found it!

Charles ran to the entrance but it was locked. On the road, there was the top of a bent stop sign. Maybe a truck ran into it and broke it off. The metal pole had been warped and twisted, appeared torn like an old chew toy at the bottom. He lifted it overhead, seeing the letters raised above him: STOP.

For a moment, he contemplated whether or not he should proceed. Was this acceptable? Breaking and entering? Stealing? Charles swallowed, felt a bead of sweat roll down, then smashed the window open and jumped in.

"Okay, okay . . . Now, what do we need."

Speaking aloud to himself seemed to calm his nerves. He took Tyler's bag from off his back, unzipped it and hurried through the aisles. He grabbed bottles of water and cans of soda, chips, candy. He grabbed some dog treats, a pack of Tylenol. There was an aluminum bat. There was a bandana.

Charles wrapped the bandana around his face to the back of his head, covering his nose and mouth. He stuck the bat in his bag, handle out.

"Well. I'm no different than 'them' now."

In the back of the store, the actual pharmacy part of the pharmacy, he found the oxygen tanks. These might have been a personal stash, he thought, belonging to the owner or one of the workers. No price tags or barcodes were visible. He found a rolling carrier next to them, one that had two slots. He checked the gauges and took the two tanks that were the most full.

"Just gotta make my way back, that's it."

The first set of turns, the now right-right-left, went smooth. It was the second set of turns that would get him.

Before his eyes, materializing in the haze, was an over-turned police car. The windows had been bashed in, the frame mangled. There were streaks of blood as if the driver had been yanked out and beaten. From behind, a figure approached. A dark and stretched silhouette hovered over him in the distorted light.

Oh, shit . . .

I don't want no trouble.

More figures appeared in front then to the side, as he

turned around, about eight or nine in total. The silhouettes danced around him, closing in.

Charles could hear the snickering, the murmurs and taunts.

Should I run for it?

The oxygen tanks in one hand, heavy backpack, it was not possible. Plus he couldn't see well enough.

"Don't come any closer."

He reached back, touched the handle of the bat as if it were a claymore sword.

"I mean it! Stay back!"

This was the decision point. Charles pulled the bat out, gripped it tight with both hands like a rookie player waiting for the pitch.

Why him? Was he just in the wrong place at the wrong time? Was it just his luck? Was it the look in his eyes? Was it the smell of him? Or did these animals not have enough yet? Still hungry, thirsty. Still crazed.

He saw the figures clearer as they drew close, ready to pounce. He faced one then the other, timing the moment to swing, to strike back.

Pop! Pop!

Pop, pop, pop!

Crackle.

Fizz.

Pop! Pop!

The fuck???

Charles and the hoodlums and hooligans shared the same startled reaction as explosions went off all around them. Some were tiny, some were huge. Some were multicolored. Some sparked up from the ground like shiny fountains.

Amongst the snapping, popping, crackling was a deep growl then a sharp bark, forming a tiny new silhouette. It scurried on all fours from along the edge then hopped on one of them, tearing at the jeans leg.

"M-Mari . . . ?"

One by one, she bit them on the hand, the leg, the forearm, until the figures started to scatter. She gave chase, hunting one of them down, jumped and bit the bastard right in the crotch—fangs clenched, pulling her snout from side to side, clawing with ferocity as she did.

He could feel the crunch of it, turned away, cringing.

Fizz.

Pop! Pop! Pop!

Crackle.

Enough force, and the bastard yanked her off, tossing her on the curb. Another one came back and kicked her in the side, rolling her over. Others joined in and stomped on her back and head.

"HEY!!!"

The fighting snarl now turned to a whimpering cry.

"YOU PIECES OF SHIT!"

Charles ran up and swung away. The firecrackers on the ground continued to build in a grand finale, as rockets flew overhead and ignited in bright bursts. Each flash lit the street, dulled the thuds and smacks of aluminum against flesh. With enough damage dealt, the rest of them took off. He watched as they fled, rubbing at their back, their thigh, their arm, their knee, their crotch.

"Mari! Mari! You okay, girl?" Bending down, he scooped her in his hands. "Oh, my God. Please. No, no, no."

Tyler walked close, the flame of the lighter still glowing. "M-Mister Charles?"

"I think they broke her rib . . ."

"Oh, crap."

The tiny dog whimpered at first, but it grew to a steady wailing.

Charles pointed to the two tanks in the rolling carrier. Tyler hobbled over and got it. Together, they walked back to the hospital in the thick haze.

Hang on, girl.

Mariana Pickle has not seen her last days.

Not here.

No, not like this.

It was the longest few blocks ever. Charles carried the limp doggy in his arms, hurting, broken. Mariana closed her eyes, the wails now weaker, a stream of tears in the black, white, goldish brown fur of her face. Tyler limped behind, his usual drag of the right leg, with the oxygen tanks rattling.

9

THE WHOLE ORDEAL lasted thirty-eight hours, though it felt like thirty-eight days. From the all caps notification to the panic to the chaos, to spreading the word and regaining back order and control. It wasn't the incompetent governor or the incompetent mayor but the very competent congresswoman who took charge and showed real strength and leadership, made the hard decisions. Although the missile threat passed—an investigation and official report was being conducted, to determine whether it was a hoax, an accident or legitimate—there was a truth revealed to the public to never be forgotten.

Serj would recover, would transition from a quad cane to a rollator.

Yanlin would give birth to a healthy baby boy, and return to her family and her family business.

Tyler would go back to playing with his fidget spinners. His grandma would give him a Scooby-Doo lunch box for his birthday.

Mariana would be just fine, as if nothing happened.

Charles would return to his regular Monday-to-Friday nine-to-five.

However, in the back of his mind, in the back of all their

minds, lingering, was the truth uncovered, that it was a matter of time. At any moment, our so-called government can crumble and fall, and allow whether through inability or unwillingness endless possibilities of devastating chain reactions.

People were scared. People were hurt. People were killed. Establishments were ransacked.

Inventory was stolen. Property was destroyed.

Someone, somewhere, at some point, could push that button: a launch, an alert, a headline, a narrative. And then it was a can of worms. The end of the world as we know it. The end of all things.

In the relative quiet, amongst the distant destruction, the crackling of flames, this concern and contemplation washed over. All of the questions, the many questions. The different ways it had gone wrong. Maybe, now, after everything, it was not too late and there was still time. One last chance. A new hope.

WASHINGTON REUNION

1

NONE OF THE graduating class from the then infamous Washington High School ever thought the memory could become so detached from their minds, but that's what happened. Over time, the gunshots muted. The sight of blood was either repressed or desensitized. For a while, for some at least, there might've been college, but there's no prom and no yearbooks. There's no hormones or acne or angst. And as degrees pile over diplomas, one gets out in the so-called real world, where many beloved classmates are taken over by a handful of beloved co-workers. Life passes in the blink of an eye. Youth is gone. No longer a kid anymore. Still as lost and alone, but expected not to be. As each weave in and out becomes each twist and turn from day to day, week to week, then over months and years, a person forgets where it all started. Friends come and go. Flames are lost and flicker away. Old wounds heal. It was easier to dream before bills and expenses. It was easier to fall in love before having to fit into a certain mold.

His reflection was faint in the oval window, and he could see the city lights far down on the ground. A slight tilt, at an angle, their slow turn in descent, until they lined up over the runway, landed and pulled in. The fasten seatbelt sign flicked off with a light chime, but he remained seated, let the others stand and retrieve their carry-on luggage first. Because once he exited that aircraft and departed from that airport, he was back home . . .

It was warmer and muggier than he was used to stepping out, crossing to the median where a line of taxis waited. An older gentleman in shirt and tie took his rolling suitcase and messenger bag, putting it in back of the van. He let the automatic door slide then hopped in the back seat, again ready to gaze out the window.

"Where we headed?" The eyes peered from the rear-view mirror.

Clearing his throat, he adjusted in place. "Over in K-Town. Just get on the freeway, I'll let you know which way."

"Oh. From here then?"

He licked his lips, nodded back.

"What high school d'you go?"

". . . Roosevelt."

There was age in his own face staring back at him from the glass. His hair was different than it had been senior year, but also there was something different behind his eyes. He leaned against the cushion, sighed to himself. *I guess I'm really back then, huh.* Which was odd because he was so dead set on leaving for such a long time, vowing to never return. Trying to escape his past, or maybe trying to escape himself, his own demons. All the thoughts bombarded his psyche, throughout the long plane ride now to the quiet cab. In the distance, he watched the cityscape glide by. The business district, uptown.

More than just buildings and businesses, a city has life of its own, and grows and changes, like a garden of concrete. So much can happen over the course of a year, over the course of multiple years. There were more homeless people in the streets living in small tent cities, after a bad economic recession hit. Violent crimes were on the rise. It seemed the public never recovered from the tragedy that happened, didn't even get the chance to, with so many things occurring in the increasingly crazy world. Scandals. Terrorism. War. Drugs. Enough time, and the Washington Massacre was a forgotten relic.

A light buzz from his pocket, he pulled out his generic smartphone and glanced at the words. Without answering, he put it away in his pocket, faced back out to the buildings whizzing past. He could almost make out the roof of the shopping center, and thought of her face, her almond eyes and her dimples, but shook the memory away.

2

SOME PAINTINGS WERE large, leaning on the walls. Most were medium sized, hanging, stacked, still drying on easels. They were everywhere. There was almost nowhere to move. He bent forward on one knee as he put finishing touches on a canvas laying right there on the floor. He threaded in streaks of neon teal and turquoise between silhouettes of figures in various poses, then turned and scanned the living room wall. By the large window, sunlight dripped through and highlighted a blank slate. Standing, he walked towards it with the brush still in hand, stepping on sheets spread out across the floor. In front of the white space, his shadow was distinct and clear, like a mirror image. On a random whim, he outlined his own shadow, which was pretty interesting. He'd never done such a thing, and wasn't sure why it occurred to him in that moment.

Before he could finish, a light buzz again, interrupting his concentration—his phone rattled on the counter of the nook in the kitchen. Putting the brush down, wiping paint off with his shirt and jeans, he hurried and answered it.

"Hey, what's up." He sat down on a stool, leaned forward. "Been a while."

"Evan. You busy? Got a minute?"

The voice on the other end was a low mumble, sounded muffled and unsure, like it always had been.

"Yeah. Just takin' a break from unpacking." He smirked, glanced around at the apartment in shambles. "Literally surrounded by boxes right now."

"Haha, okay, cool. Just wanted to make sure we're still on for tonight—"

"Should be."

"—and I was too lazy to text all the info, so I just called. Old school, I know."

There was a pause. In the short silence, he noticed one box in particular that caught his eye.

"It starts like ten, but maybe we could meet a little earlier around nine? The show'll be at The Hub. You know where?"

"Yup. I remember. It used to be Space Station, right?"

"That's the one. Uh, anyone else coming?"

"Nah. The others are all busy so just us two."

"Pussies."

Both of them laughed, kind of like when they were younger.

"We'll meet at the old karaoke spot first, yeah?

"Okay, sounds good."

"Ah, all right. I'll let ya go then."

"Cool, Max. See you tonight."

He pressed the icon on the screen, laid the phone back down, then stared at the one box again. It was strange hearing from his old friend after all that time. Both had changed. The world around them had changed. Yet, whatever forces there were brought them back together again.

On impulse, he stepped toward the crooked column of boxes, taking off the top layers and holding the one that beckoned him. He took out an old discman with cheap headphones, a couple CDs, a composition book and mechanical pencil, then an object wrapped in cloth. Unwinding the fabric, holding it tight in his hand, the blade of the knife was dull through circular holes in the handle. As he felt the edge of the knife with his thumb and fingertips, his mind began to wander . . .

3

Jan 20th
12:48am

LONG RIBBONS OF yellow police tape flickered in the soft breeze. After crowds prayed and held hands, hugging and singing songs . . . After so many lit candles glowed and cards of mourning scattered along the back fence . . . Evan returned to the literal scene of the crime. There was a faint blue light on the far side of campus, which he assumed was a cop car on patrol. He ducked low and strafed the pillars between buildings A through D, until he was inside the administration building. In the pitch black, he could still make out round holes dug into the concrete as well as blackened streaks. The fountain was half-stuck in the on position, dripping from the bowl. The glass from the vending machine cracked in an elaborate spiderweb design. A puddle of blood remained where he had found Max on the ground.

Evan stopped, felt a slight shiver down his spine to his stomach as every hair on his arm tingled. The images flashed in his mind: shallow breaths, the whites of the eyes bulged, torso stained dark crimson. The sounds replayed: a gasping wheeze, sharp hisses and raspy coughs, choking with a gurgling noise.

He forced himself forward, feeling his eyes tear up. The gate to the stairwell was still chained and locked. As he walked down the east wing towards F-building, he swallowed a dry lump of air. Stepping up the inner stairs, he could hear her voice distinct and clear.

What if . . .

What if I want to be with you too?

In his hand was a single rose, and it dangled down in the darkness. Evan made his way back across the walkway to the second floor of admin. He stood in front of the library doors, which automatically whooshed open. Although he was prepared to break in if he had to, he was glad that wasn't the case. With everything that happened, of course it went unnoticed.

Aiming the flashlight, he felt nervous. He was still in shock, still couldn't believe all that occurred. The authorities had been through the area, cleaned up some, but there were still torn pages strewn about the floor. Feeling like a ghost hunter investigating an alleged haunted location, he walked forward despite his instincts not to. As the light cut through the dark, shadows stretched and warped like demonic talons. A chill ran down his spine to his tailbone.

Stepping past the turnstile and sensor, he could see the marble counter. Evan placed the flashlight down sideways so that it illuminated the open space. As it clicked and slid on the countertop, he remembered the AR-15 and the gas mask that had been there . . .

Bang.

Bang, bang, bang.

He flinched and turned away, away from the flashback, glancing around at the tables. Some were turned over, some were broken. There was an outline on the floor that resembled a scarecrow where his best friend had taken his last breath. A marker of where the gun had ended up lay right next to it. Together, side by side, they appeared like a large continent with a smaller neighboring island.

"Derek . . ."

Kneeling down, he laid the rose over the scarecrow's chest. Then he traced a trail of blood to a broken table by one of the slanted shelves.

Evan sniffled, took a deep breath. "Der, I . . ."

Shaking his head, shutting his eyes, he walked to the table, adjusted his one arm in a sling. In the darkness, he could make out a slight shimmer. How was it still there? Did they not see it, not take it into evidence? Maybe it was meant for him to find. To be his, to have and to hold. To be haunted by. It wasn't his intention to retrieve it, no, not at all, but that he did. That moment, with the butterfly knife in hand, his best friend had returned from the dead.

4

No FIRE DRILL could have prepared them for that day, for what was to come. It was a horrific tragedy, years in the making. Although the world had changed, they right along with it, some things remained just as that very day. Like the scar on his back, which became a part of him, a sign he carried with him a deep hole. That hole followed him, and he could never escape. The boy who lived. For a long while in the healing process, it remained reddish brown, the surrounding flesh sore to the touch, but over time, it became skin color once again, just a tad paler white. Now, putting on a collar shirt over an undershirt, buttoning in the mirror, Evan couldn't see it. Out of sight, out of mind. Another forgotten relic.

His reflection stared back at him as he walked toward it. Then he and his reflection walked together side by side as he turned, passed by glass panes alongside the building to the front entrance. A valet left the stool and podium as a luxury car pulled up. If it were still high school, they would have met at the comic book shop or the arcade, maybe go over to some-body's house. But it had been almost ten years. In fifth grade, the playground was in the dirt next to the one big tree. Then, from prepubescence to adolescence, that so-called playground turns into the mall and movie theater, to the opposite sex. In young adulthood, it becomes more settings like this: bars, clubs, restaurants.

The lobby had a sitting area, front desks for checking in and assistance. There were a couple restaurants off to one side, a coffee shop, an escalator going up to the parking garage. On the other side was the spot he was looking for, with a stairs hidden that led down a level, off the beaten path.

As he entered, Evan spotted Max right away, sitting at a table near the corner of the bar. He had his usual awkward smile as he lifted the mug and took a good swig. His hair was long and grown out, past shoulder length, and he had a thick mustache and goatee beard. He wore a fedora hat and a graphic tee.

Evan raised his arms, joined his old friend, clapping palms together then leaning over for a bro hug.

"Hey, dude. Long time no see."

Max snorted, leaned back in the wheelchair. "'Sup."

"Lemme get a drink real quick."

After ordering a gin and tonic, dropping tip on the bar top, he turned back to go sit with Max. In the short time he stood at the bar, a couple people went over to talk to him. He must have been a regular there, 'cause they treated him with a certain level of admiration and respect, as if he was a kind of celebrity.

Evan smirked to himself. As he drew closer, they left Max to go to the side of the L-shaped bar.

"Man. Pretty famous now, huh?"

They each raised their drink, clinked their glasses together.

"Cheers. Been a hella long time since Wash."

Over the years, they'd kept in touch. The occasional hangout, smaller parties and get-togethers, like a rock show or a spontaneous road trip upstate. Not as often as when they were young, when their whole world revolved around the lopsided polygon that was their group.

"So, what the hell you been up to?"

Max chuckled. "Shit . . ."

"Last time I seen you, we were both about to move."

"Yeah, yeah. That's right." He took a slow sip. "Um, let's see. I just kind of went out and about, you know? On a spiritual journey of sorts."

Evan swilled his glass, ice cubes clinking as he listened.

"I went to California. I went to New York. Partied my way down the coast for a while there, spent a semester abroad."

Damn. You made it before me . . .

"College was fun for a bit but then I looked up and kinda realized I became this 'super senior' of sorts. Ya know? Just doing class after class, for the hell of it. I decided to take off, travel. A couple months ago, I moved home to help my mom who's getting older."

"How is your mom?"

"Ah, fuck that bitch." He let out a hyena laugh. "Sick of her ass already."

Evan smirked, forced a laugh, although it was disingenuous.

"What about you? I figured you and what's-her-face woulda got hitched by now, together a long time. You guys moved together, right?"

"Yeah, we were. But it just didn't work out."

"That sucks, dude." He leaned forward, lifted his mug for another cheers to which Evan reciprocated.

Behind the facial hair and the long straggly hair, beneath the fedora hat, was his old friend. The same kid he saw get bullied, who was pale and skinny, with braces and bad acne . . . The same kid unsure of his step, who said and did strange things that were alarming, downright disturbing at times . . . Had things been different, it could've been him that went down a bad road, easy. Maybe it wasn't a kabuki mask or a mask from a masquerade ball, but this new look was a sort of "mask" in itself. And the mug in his hand a deadly weapon also.

At least he's doing better than before.

Max let out a proud belch, touched the brim of his hat, played with his beard. "Um. Did ya hear about the reunion?"

"Oh, no. . . . Wow. Has it been that long?"

"Right? Like, we're old men already."

Evan squeezed his lemon wedge before taking a chug. "I guess I'll have to think that over. I mean, not like any of us are dying to relive those memories."

"Plus I'm sure the press will turn it into some kinda publicity stunt or some shit. Frickin' greedy-ass vultures."

"Right off the bat, I do kinda wanna say, yeah, I'll probably be interested. For some reason. Not even sure why."

Max shook his head. "Sadly, me too."

"Like, as much as we all wanna escape . . . it's a part of us. Part of our past, part of our souls. Etched in, like carvings on a wood desktop."

Evan imagined being back in an empty classroom, facing a blank chalkboard. The desk in front of him had a heart drawn with letters written in.

E

+

J

It brought a slight smirk to his face, until he saw there was a spent shell casing on the floor. When he stared back up, it became the stage from the auditorium. The quiet space. Curtains pulled. Stage lights shining at varying angles.

He was all alone. No kid in uniform, no kid with the bandaged hand. There was no short girl with glasses or girl with droopy eyes. No goth, no gangsta.

". . . W-what you drinkin', Max? I'll get us another round." Evan already began to stand from the table.

"Sure. Just one, though. This is just pre-game."

Not unlike the etching in the desk, his heart also had an arrow through it. Every now and then, he could still feel it lodged. He breathed in and out as he turned to go to the bar.

As they went through the busy streets, which were roaring and rowdy, Evan and Max weaved in between bodies and streetlights and stands with pamphlets and flyers, the occasional garbage can. Some women wore sleek tight dresses that hugged their curves. Groups of men were dressed in slim fit button-downs, a good number just military in town. Evan smirked to himself as he took it all in, being back, being out and about. Max pressed his gloved palms up the rims of the wheelchair with expert timing and technique, rolling down the crosswalk and up the small incline in the curb. He bent forward with a slight hunch, his awkward smile stretched wide. It was clear Max had found his true self, embraced this identity: the hippie, wild man, party animal.

From one end of the lane, a straight shot across the shops and restaurants of the beachfront, with hotels on either side, the two made their way to the rock show. Once a Month Punk, it was called.

They paid the small fee, got the wristbands, and joined the crowd smushed together in front of the stage. Just in time as the band plugged in their cords and pedals, reverberating through the multiple amps, tapped at the microphone and did a mic-check-one-two. The lights shined in diagonals across the different members, the guitarist, the drummer, the bass, the lead. With the welcome words from the vocalist, the crowd cheered and shouted.

A tick, tick, tick, tick of the drumsticks then the guitar riff and bass line collided together in a blend of static and noise. Right away, the lead jumped up and screamed into the mic, sending a raspy guttural wave through the speaker system. Banging their heads up and down to the rhythm, rocking their bodies with it, the energy flowed through them all. This grew in momentum until there was a circular mini-mosh pit forming that shoved and bumped into one another like a peace rally turned riot. Max took his hat off and rolled his neck to the music, sending his long hair in a perfect centrifugal spiral, to which the area around him screamed—his signature move.

Evan cupped one hand, yelled through to Max's ear. "I'm gonna get a drink!"

"Whaaat?"

"I'm gonna go, get, a drink!"

Max nodded, shifted back towards the show that continued. Squeezing from the mini-mosh pit through the packed crowd behind where it was more thinned out, Evan turned side to side and tiptoed. In the short line, he caught his breath and relaxed. Leaning against the wall, there was a girl with a drink in her hand, like a wallflower. She was in conversation with a friend, both talking, almost indifferent to their surroundings. For a moment, the two locked eyes but Evan faced away, instead gazed down at the ground, unsure why.

He ordered, this time a vodka tonic and another bottle for Max, dropped tip in the jar then headed back. A drink in each hand, Evan was careful making his way back to the front, through the crowd bouncing and thrashing to the more upbeat song. He handed it to Max, they each cheers'd, then turned back to the stage and nodded along.

As the night tore on, song after song, band after band—even though they were tired, even though they were buzzed—they rocked to the music blaring. Towards the other side of the stage, there was the wallflower again, with two friends, the same girl and now some guy. The last time he went to go get a drink, he noticed she and her friend had gone. She seemed more interested in observing the action versus participating in it. Across the moving bodies and the flashing lights, their eyes met. Evan stared back, for a second, then forced himself to watch the show and not glance in her direction.

When the singer of the last band announced it was all over, thank you and good night, the crowd shouted and chanted demanding more. Now a full-blown mosh pit raged out of control. Max raced along counterclockwise, around the inner wall of the maelstrom. Evan tried backing away, but someone shoved him from behind into the chaos. He got rammed into, spilling his drink all onto his shirt, sending little blocks of ice sliding across the linoleum floor.

Ah, shit . . .

Are you frickin' serious . . .

He stepped through what was left of the crowd, dripping wet, to one of the tables in the standing area.

Max followed, laughing. "Haha. Party foul."

"Damn it. Worst part is that cost me like six bucks."

"You all right?"

"Yeah, just—"

Another voice chimed in. "Y'guys okay? That was crazy, I saw the whole thing."

Evan turned around to the wallflower and her friends.

"Here." She offered a wad of napkins, already started dabbing the front of his shirt. "We just ate before we came, and they gave us way too many napkins."

"I like your moves. You're crazy." The guy from afar appeared like a frat boy, but up close spoke in a higher register and had effeminate mannerisms. "That hair, tho."

"For real!"

Max let out his hyena laugh, leaning back. "I know, right."

"Thanks." Evan swallowed, scanning her eyes.

Her eyelids fluttered as her lips stretched in a thin smile. "Sorry, this is probably awkward."

She dabbed down lower, from his chest to his stomach.

"J-just the shirt . . ."

"Oh. Sorry."

They both laughed, shifted toward the others.

"You guys wanna go somewhere else? After party? We know a place where the bartender can hook us up."

"Yeah, sure."

Damn it, Max.

The wallflower smiled at him, and they all made their way.

Although he was reluctant, Evan understood to go with the flow. That was the true joy of going out and partying. Never knowing who you might meet, where you might end up. It's best to take that chance and live it up. Max had become more and more like this over the years, kind of spontaneous, kind of crazy in fact, always literally and metaphorically rolling with it. Seize the night. Carpe noctem.

Just down the block, upstairs, around the side to a balcony with hanging lights, they sat down at a round table. It was quieter and nice. The bartender came over and greeted Max. Again, it was like he was a little celebrity.

"So, how come you're in a wheelchair?"

The one girl shoved the guy with her elbow, glared.

"What? Bitch. I'm just asking."

"Nah, nah, it's cool." Max leaned in. "I was actually in the Washington Massacre, shot in the back."

The partiers grew quiet, a couple drew sharp breaths and covered their mouths. Evan shook his head, faced away.

"He was too. Got stabbed."

Max . . .

Evan gave him a look, bit down on his lower lip.

"Is that true?" The wallflower leaned close. "Oh, God."

"Yeah, long time ago now. It's old news. I mean, there's been how many shootings since."

The one girl hesitated, then continued. "I have an aunt that works in the school system, higher up, says a lot of what happened was due to police negligence, that many of the injuries and deaths could have been avoided."

"I don't know. Hard to say. Phone lines were cut, and there was that big fire on the freeway overpass as a diversion, causing backed up traffic. And one of the first times anything like that ever happened, really."

"What was it like?" The wallflower asked, with a somber face.

Slouching with his arms folded, Max exhaled. "Uh. You wanna tell 'em, Evan?"

You're killing me, man.

He cleared his throat. "Well. It's almost . . . surreal or something. Like, when you first see it, blood, I swear it doesn't even look like blood. It kinda seems like red paint or something. Something 'normal,' you know?"

Each of them grew quiet, some diverting their eyes downward.

Pausing for a moment, Evan then continued, dazing off.

"And when you first hear gunshots, it sounds like . . .

like fireworks, or a car backfire. You might feel scared for a moment, maybe, but most of all you don't feel, period. It's either an adrenaline thing or you just accept it."

The tension in the air was thick like smog.

"Okay, who needs a shot."

"Haha, 'shot' . . . Get it?"

Max turned, raised five fingers. "Tequila. Salt, lime."

Everyone else laughed along to the borderline inappropriate joke, but Evan kept quiet, still lingering in that place he tried so hard to forget, to escape.

As the night continued, that moment passed. There was another round, along with finger food. There was drunken darts, with some attempts bouncing hard on the floor, or missing the dartboard altogether and becoming lost. One of the girls had an apartment nearby so they migrated towards it as a final nightcap. Evan was sobering up by that point but still tried to be the proper wingman, back Max up since he wanted to keep going. The guy and the girl took the lead, stumbling, one arm around one another's shoulder. Max followed, zigzagging then doing a spin move. Evan was quiet, gazed down at his feet with his hands in his pockets. The wallflower slid her wrist in between his right arm and his side, clinging around at his inner elbow. He turned and forced a smirk. Her eyes glistened as she smiled, squeezed, then nudged closer.

"Gimme your phone."

He obliged, handed it over. She put in her info, reached across his torso, dropping the smartphone back in his pocket.

It was a cute move. A sweet voice, a sweet laugh. Her hair was a darker, dirty blonde with highlights. Just a tasteful sliver of cleavage from her tight shirt hugging around her chest beneath her vintage jacket, and her jeggings covered her smooth legs in a perfect fit. All in all, this was a real nice girl and it seemed Evan had scored the jackpot. Yet, somehow he felt nothing, nothing more than basal male instinct.

Evan had experienced this many times before. Meeting a girl, finding a girl. And for some reason, there just wasn't any spark. Instead, he would think of *her* . . . The one that got away. His mind would ruminate and compare and calculate, would dwell. Her eyes weren't as nice, maybe. Her hair didn't have this sort of shimmery sheen in the morning light. She didn't have dimples. She wasn't smart enough. Then, in time, he would go on to regret it, then reconsider, and ruminate and dwell again.

The guy and girl went into the kitchen, took out some glasses. Max rolled into the living room, settled between the La-Z-Boy and the dinner table. Evan and the wallflower followed, sat on the sofa.

He glanced at the clock, setting a time limit to when he would call it quits.

"You havin' a good time?" His mumble mixed with a slur, one palm on the wheel.

"Yeah, dude. Always good catching the rock shows with you, punk to metal. Us and our shenanigans, right?"

Max motioned with his chin. Evan shifted, realized the wallflower closed her eyes and rested her cheek against his arm. She breathed in and out with a slow breath. He smirked then stared out the window to the tall buildings.

For a moment, Evan thought of the good ol' days. He pictured the day of the sleepover and sitting on Derek's bed, pictured the stairwell in F-building where *she* did the exact same thing but which he did feel a spark. A powerful spark he couldn't deny or try to dissect and explain. This "spark" left a deep impression on him like the scar on his back.

After he snuck away, gave a soft hug to the sleepy wallflower, waved goodbye to the others and bumped fists with Max, Evan walked through the streets alone. He thought about how different things had become over the years. Max with his long hair and facial hair, his fedora. Construction sites on the other side of the street furthered gentrification and catering to the tourists. They used to play video games, they used to watch cartoons, and now they took shots and went out to bars. Their high school experience was now a topic of conversation, of debate. Between moving and the breakup, he felt so lost, so out of touch—out of his own time.

5

With one eye open, in a small sticky puddle of saliva, Evan shuddered awake. He rolled to his side and sat on the edge of the bed. Arching his head back, he yawned and stretched. There was a light headache starting to kick in so he went to the kitchen to hydrate before the hangover got too bad. As he passed through, all the boxes, the paintings and paint supplies, all of the clothing and household items, it reminded him of the chores that needed to get done. Yet, of course, the very first thing Evan did was nothing at all. Procrastinate, as he plopped down on the end of the small couch, sitting sideways, placing his bulky laptop on the armrest. He unfolded it to a light chime as it lagged, turned on and loaded.

During high school, the information super highway was just starting to roll out into the mainstream. Now, it was pretty much everything. A way to check information like the news or the weather, to register for events or apply for jobs, to order items. From a screen in the living room to a screen on the go, inside of pockets, to the palm of one's hand. Anything anybody can think of, there's an app for that. It was how to connect to people, and how to keep in touch.

A click and a scroll away, the single person lingering at

the back of his subconscious appeared before him. Not the ex he had just broken up with, not even the wallflower from last night, no. The original, the first. Corner of the isosceles triangle. Eye of the tornado that once swept him up.

There she was, beautiful, serene, exuberant. With her smile so deep it cut dimples in her cheeks. Her almond eyes lit up as the simple background illuminated her in that candid moment. Evan clicked on picture after picture, mesmerized, yearning. It was like she was a celestial being on a different plane of existence.

He could still remember the smell of her perfume. Could still remember the taste of her lip gloss. Still remembered her pretty fingernail and her bracelets when they first shared a textbook between them in class. Her hand sliding onto his as they moved the mouse in the computer lab. Behind the curtain before the talent show. At the movie theater, at the shopping center. Sitting on the sideways tree trunk feeding the ducks. Up high above the carnival, dreaming of all of the possibilities of their lives before them.

Unlike so many forgotten relics throughout the course of his life, the memory of her was instead a kept treasure.

Evan closed the laptop, glanced around, again knew what needed to be done but just couldn't bring himself to do it quite yet. He instead grabbed a paintbrush and palette, walked to the nearest empty canvas and easel.

First, he slathered a layer of titanium white over the white of the canvas for "wet on wet." There were many techniques he liked to incorporate, but the alla prima method was iconic. He painted the background a phthalo blue, leaving a rounded blank space in the middle that he then outlined in the shape of a heart, filling it in alizarin crimson. As he streaked over the right side in an upward diagonal motion, Evan blurred the clear cut lines with pinks and purples, waves of yellow and orange like fire.

6

THE CERAMIC CUP was nice and warm, its raised design pleasant against his fingertips. His eyes stared at the green tea and the bits of leaves at the bottom. Evan was more than happy to be in this familiar setting. His last city didn't quite have the same taste or smell in the food, didn't have the same feel in the places. He reached and grabbed chopsticks, removing the paper wrapper and folding it, tapped the end of it then split it open. The movement and sound reminded him of how he used to bang his mechanical pencil on his composition book like a drumstick to kill time. Some things never change. Through the double doors out front, he could see Mark walk in, with his wide grin and squinty eyes.

When he got closer, they stood and clapped palms and hugged. Mark was in a collar shirt with floral print and black slacks. Evan noticed the dazed look in his eye, the little stubbles on his chin.

"Dude. You all right? Seem exhausted."

"Tax season now. Just got out the office." He shook his head, leaned back with arms folded. "Fuck . . ."

Mark was the first of all of them to get a real job, already received an offer before he even finished his last semester. He worked hard, graduated on time with a double major, did the proper networking in the proper clubs and organizations. Evan was still taking college courses when Mark prepped for his CPA exam and they would often study together at some all-night fast food spot.

"Good to see you. Sucks about breaking up, but good to see you."

"Ah, it's okay. I'm back on the rock now."

"How'd you like living up there, anyway?" His ears perked up as he adjusted against the back cushion.

Evan leaned forward on one elbow, sipped the tea. "Cold. Rainy."

They both laughed.

"Nah, but seriously, I did like it. Y'know, the coffee shops and boutiques and hipster people, trees. All of it. It was so cool and so unique. Very grunge."

"Sounds like you. How was last night, with Max?"

"It wasn't too bad. I mean, he's doing a lot better than those last few times I partied with him, I'll say that. You remember, right?"

Mark nodded.

"Passing out, blacking out, puking. Breaking down and yelling at the top of his lungs. Borderline crying right in front of me. There were times I was legit scared he had alcohol poisoning . . ." Evan faced Mark, whose usual wide grin was long gone. "He seems pretty good now, though. Like in a good place. Mentally."

"No more talk about trying to off himself?"

"Nah. He seemed okay."

"Cool, cool." Mark took a gulp of ice water, swallowed. "I mean, you know he's not my favorite person. In fact, I mostly find him kinda weird and annoying."

Evan smirked, shook his head.

"But I wouldn't wish that upon anybody, no way. We all been through enough, more than most people."

The waitress hovered over, offered to take their order, but they each said they would wait. She was cute, pleasant, with glasses and her hair up, a few bangs hanging down, slight curves showing through her polo shirt beneath her apron. Both made a subtle face to one another—mild in comparison to the way they behaved in high school, when checking out girls was their primary hobby.

Next to them on the rotating belt, a parade of various sushi floated by. Evan liked to sit in a position where he could see what was coming around the bend, steady towards their booth. The plates were clean, nori wrapped neat, with cuts of fish sliced at the perfect angle, set on rounded beds of rice.

Grabbing a container of wasabi from the belt, Mark took a dollop and placed it on his saucer. Evan did the same then returned it. They each poured soy sauce. Mark mixed his into a greenish brown paste that was thick, sure to be spicy. Evan mixed some, leaving the chunk of bright green and adding a piece of pink ginger, for just a touch of spice.

"Oh, man. It's good to be home, at least in this way." Evan licked his lips, took a deep breath. "Somethin' about sitting down at this place. Know what I mean?"

"For sure. Me, too. Actually haven't been here in a while. But I thought we'd come down for ol' time sake."

As Mark slouched and relaxed, Evan leaned on one elbow.

"So, I know we sometimes like to meet early, but there any reason you wanted to? Not sure why but I got this funny feeling . . ."

Mark grinned. "All this time and you still can just tell, huh?"

"Dude, you can't deny the bromance."

Both of them howled in laughter, perhaps a little too loud.

"No, you're right." Mark cleared his throat, paused, continued. "I actually, uh, asked Kelly to marry me."

"Did you she say yes???"

"Yeah, hehe. Against her better judgment."

Evan stood again, walked around to the side of the booth. Mark also stood, and they each hugged a nice long hug. He then shook Mark at the shoulders, hit him on the side of the arm.

"Are you serious!? That's frickin' great."

They both sat back down, slid back inside.

"Oh, and uh . . . You're my best man."

"Whaat? Awesome. I'm shocked."

"I mean, me too, but it's just about time. Getting up there, you know?"

Such a funny thing to say, but compared to when they were teenagers, they were now ancient beings. Time seemed to pass at different rates at different stages of life. When they were little, wrestling and playing pretend, it was as if it stood still, not even nudging an inch. In adolescence, it stretched on and on, sometimes taking forever. And now, in young adulthood, it started to pick up pace to the point that moments can flash so quick.

Evan sighed. "I like Kelly—"

"I know you do, a little too much."

"Shut up! It's *her*, not me!"

This was an old and ongoing joke, innocent. He gazed at his friend then, traced over the slight wrinkles in his forehead and the crow's feet developing around his eyes, and smirked to himself. It was a genuine pleasure for Evan to see Mark in such a good place. He didn't realize how much this meant to him until then, but from every forced double date to every nudge, push and shove to go and hit on a girl or to ask a girl out, at last, his friend had made it through to the other side. Happy for him was an understatement.

"All right, lemme text Jar. See where he's at. 'Cause I'm ready to eat . . ."

So much to say, but Evan just let out a quiet chuckle along with a small shake of his head, crossing his arms.

"He's almost here. Couple more minutes." Mark squirmed in place, put his phone back in his pocket. "But yeah, thanks for coming a little early. I wanted to tell you that and ask you that, catch up a bit before."

"No prob."

"Don't say anything yet. I'll tell him later. Not sure yet if I'm gonna ask him to be a groomsman or what. Kelly knows more about this stuff, so I'm playing it by ear. Speaking of, I better check in . . ."

He began to squirm again, reached back into his pocket.

"Aw, man. Never thought I'd see the day."

Mark grinned. "What?"

"You're so pussy-whipped."

"Dude. I been pussy-whipped since before I even saw a pussy."

This led to both of them bawling, hunched over and gasping for air. When they calmed and caught their breath, Mark shook his head, held his glass in his hand.

"You know, it's funny that I'm first to get engaged. Really, I always thought it would be you. Hell, we all thought it would be."

"I . . ." Evan swallowed a dry lump. "I thought it would be too."

A short awkward silence ensued, allowing his mind to

wander. Evan had also experienced this many times. Ruminating, calculating, dwelling. Regrets. Wondering when did this become his life? Wondering if it was too late. Wondering, at what point, did something go terribly wrong?

From the double doors out in front, Jared made his way down. He clapped palms with them one by one, then sat on the side of the booth by Evan. The waitress came and took their orders.

Mark widened his eyes, raised his eyebrows and sat up straight. "Can I have a tobiko and spicy tuna?"

Evan chimed in. "Make that two spicy tunas."

"Two spicy tunas, one salmon." Mark counted with his fingers.

"A salmon skin roll."

The two almost had their orders down to a science.

Mark faced Evan. "That's it for now, I think. Anything else?"

"Chicken karaage."

The waitress turned to Jared, who lifted a hand up. "I'll just take miso soup, and one more karaage."

She nodded, scribbled it all down.

"Oh, and a Coke."

Evan and Mark laughed a hushed laugh amongst themselves, covering their mouths. When the waitress turned away, they let it out.

Jared shook his head, staring at his two idiot friends.

"We all knew it was coming."

"Of course the Coke, but you only got those two things?" Evan asked, leaning his cheek in his palm, elbow on the table.

"I don't like fish. How many times I gotta tell you guys."

"Oh, that's right." Mark arched his neck back, shuddering in place from the laughter. "I completely forgot."

"Well, you don't have to eat it, I guess . . ." Evan tried to fix it.

Jared shook his head again. "I don't like the sight of fish, I don't like the smell of fish. I don't know why you asses always insist on coming here."

The two turned to each other and laughed, Mark slapping a hand to his knee and falling over sideways.

"Hey. I did suggest curry." Evan again tried to fix it.

"I fuckin' hate you guys."

All laughed this time, then quieted. Jared leaned on his elbows, interlacing his fingers, slouched. Mark gulped his water, which was half gone by then. Evan stared at his two best friends, one then the other, and smirked to himself. One now starting to show wrinkles, and one now a few pounds heavier. No matter what was going on in his life, at least he always had this: the boys, his boys. Here they all were, back together again after so many long years, still the three stooges, still the three musketeers.

Each small circular plate stacked, started to form matching piles around them. Jared took his time nibbling piece after piece of edamame from the shell. Mark ordered a few more, Evan just a couple more. He swilled the last of his green tea, watching it ripple, quiet, waiting for the opportune moment to bring up what was on his mind. They always had their fun, were good at being silly and making jokes, but tended to avoid most serious conversations, even more so as they grew older. Evan breathed in and out, became contemplative gazing to the front area where a teen boy and a teen girl paid their bill then walked out, hand in hand. Through the glass panel, he could see them smiling.

"So . . . Know what I just heard . . ."

Jared turned to him. "What?"

Mark's mouth was full, his chewing pronounced. "Yeah, what."

"I guess, h-has it been ten years? It's our reunion coming up."

"Oh, no shit." Jared raised his brows, jutted out his lower lip. "That's so crazy. What the hell happened?"

"Reunion . . ." Mark wore a blank expression. "Why do we even need a reunion? Got everybody on social, on messenger. I hear from too many assholes as it is."

"Ha, not me."

Jared shook his head with a slight chuckle. He was one of the few people left who never did make any online accounts, would never be caught dead taking a selfie or being tagged in a group pic. Never did post, never did share. Probably never liked or commented. Jared was also still a bachelor and seemed content to be.

"You guys gonna go?"

"Ah, maybe." Tilting his head to one side, Jared lifted his glass and sipped his soda through the straw. "I'll think about it, I guess. Mark has a super good point, though. Like ten, twenty years ago, reunions made sense because you lost touch, were probably curious. Now, well, you're still in touch."

"Right." Mark chimed in, a slight glare setting in. "And it's already annoying reading people's dumb posts, debating whether or not to accept their dumb requests. Do I really need to pay fifty bucks to see someone I see on my feed all day every damn day, that I don't even wanna see? That I don't even like???"

A small round of laughter between them.

"Especially, like, we all got jobs. There's only so many

hours of free time in a day, in a week . . ." Jared cracked his knuckles. "And you're not one of 'em."

Mark snorted, faced Evan from across the table. "How about you?"

"I dunno." Evan glanced downward, leaned back. "Like, I'm not opposed to the idea, no. A little curious, in fact. But at the same time, not sure I wanna go back down that road too."

Then, he grew quiet. His two friends did the same, in a spontaneous moment of shared silence.

He didn't tell them everything that happened. It was shocking enough their former best friend they all lost touch with turned out to be one of the shooters, let alone the one that planned it. How could he tell them about the confrontation in the library? How could he tell them the truth of how he got stabbed? All of the things said. Every punch, every kick. Holding Derek in his arms as he bled out on the carpet. He just couldn't do that to them after everything they already suffered. Mark would've pissed on Derek's grave if he knew. Whatever little pity and wholesome memory Jared held onto would be tainted and ruined forever.

There was just a single person who knew, who he did tell. One of many secrets between the two star-crossed hearts like threads of silk.

7

IT WAS DARK out, cold. Not sure why, but he couldn't fall asleep. Maybe it was a little too much food at dinner with the guys or maybe it was the hangover hitting him now in a delay. He tossed and turned, rolled over, until he got up and walked through the darkened apartment, plopped down on the couch. At first, Evan took out his smartphone and clicked and scrolled. When he came across the wallflower in his contacts, he stopped and hovered, stared. Not that he would call or text her then—no, not at that hour—but he thought about her then. Her hair, her face. Her voice. She was cute. She was cool. Yet, again, there just wasn't any spark there, or not enough of one. He took a deep breath, sighed to himself. As he did this, his eyes adjusted in the dark enough that he could see the bulky laptop on the armrest still.

He reached over, unfolded it to a light chime. As it lagged and loaded, he thought of *her* instead. A small flutter built up from the pit of his stomach to his chest, then out through his bones, to his fingertips, to his teeth . . .

It was something he hadn't felt in a long, long time. Evan paused, noticed it himself for a brief moment, blinked then continued, opening the social media site. There she was again, glowing in the pitch black around him. She brightened all the paintings at once. The curtains, the boxes. The walls, the floor. A soft light that blended shadow with dim muted color. Now, the small flutter turned into a small implosion.

Memories of her flashed—from prom, from the talent show. Her playing the piano, glancing back across at him. The two of them slow dancing, with the stage lights angled down and across their faces. And then the light of the moon as they rolled in the sand, fumbled unbuttoning, and heavy breathing and heavy pawing against the gentle splashing of the waves.

As Evan gazed into her digital eyes on the screen, he longed for her like he did back then when he held her at the waist, when they lay on the grass in the park with their fingers interlocked.

He forced himself to turn away, faced down, swallowing dry air.

What . . . the hell . . . am I doing?

Before he could even process his own question, he already clicked away until all the pictures were there before him again in cyberspace. Evan traced them and scanned them, each beautiful still from a life he was unfamiliar with. Her perfect imperfection captured in a frozen laugh, with her dimples peeking through and her eyes with a slight shimmer.

The pointer arrow slid across the screen and hovered over a Send Message button, almost like involuntary muscle movement. Evan felt detached from his own body in that instant, as if he could see the reflection of the screen in his own eyes. He closed them, blinked, breathed, then clicked.

A blank white square and a blinking cursor awaited.

Dear Jude,

8

10 Months Later

ON A LADDER turned sideways, Evan hovered over the large canvas where he continually stroked the brush. Side to side and then crisscross in a diagonal X pattern, he let his wrist blend the colors onto the blank slate, the magic of turning nothing into something. In the middle of that process of creation and perception, then inspiration and creation once again, he worked. His shoulder was sore from working at that angle, but it was still better than upright. When he finished that section, he crawled off the ladder and grabbed a paint can. He used a flat-head screwdriver to pop the top open then went over to a different canvas, spilling fresh paint in a long snaking swirl then pouring it at the bottom for a splash effect. Last, Evan took a paint sprayer and splotched and splattered it in a curved outward motion.

The interior was more tidy, but cluttered with easels and palettes and other art supplies in a kind of organized chaos. He stepped away, wiped some of the paint onto his pants before plopping down on the couch. Evan glanced at the clock on the wall, then closed his eyes with a deep breath.

Am I really ready for this?

It might have been a long few months since he first heard about the upcoming reunion, but the truth was that it had been a long decade before that in his life which seemed stagnant. Not just going back to that period in time, but back to those old faces, old places, old events—that specific one that loomed over each of them like a dark, thick, heavy rain cloud.

Was he ready to think about gunshots again? Was he ready to think about shooters again, about victims again? Ready to think about the death count, which raised in tally to twenty-four after the final unfortunate soul ended up passing at the hospital after clinging on for almost a full week.

Evan couldn't help thinking about those certain details from time to time, like how authorities and reports stated the shooters took their own lives. But he knew that wasn't true, at least not all of them. He was supposed to live, to remember, to suffer, and then find some kinda meaning in the suffering.

While getting dressed at a very sluggish and reluctant pace, Evan pondered all this. He glanced in the mirror, took a deep breath, shook out his fingers and tilted his neck. The vibration in his pocket meant Mark was downstairs, waiting, and it was time, ready or not, like it or not.

"Hey, dude. Thanks for picking me up." Evan climbed in, reached a hand out.

Mark grinned, leaned over as they clapped palms. "It's cool. Again, I'll be leaving early so you're on your own after that. Gotta wipe your own ass."

"I'll figure something out, haha."

The two old friends, in the messy white Prius, on the drive from K-Town to the business district, were unknowingly on a journey through time and space. On the surface, they were technically twenty-somethings but soon would be like teenagers all over.

"I said it once and I'll say it again. 'Should've went to Roosevelt.' Fuck."

Both laughed. Mark covered his mouth, rotating the wheel, while Evan slapped at his knee, leaning back into the seat.

An inside joke they often referred to. Evan should never have transferred. And, even Mark was pushed by his family to go to Roosevelt instead of Washington. It must have been fate that they both ended up at the now infamous school, and would be branded as an Eagle for all eternity.

"So, no Jar, huh? Really didn't come."

"Nah. Too anti for this kinda thing. Got issues. Hell, I don't even wanna frickin' go either so I don't blame him."

"Hey, we all got issues."

Mark signaled then switched lanes.

"You said Max was gonna meet us there?"

"Yeah."

"Well, this is it. The big day. You all right?"

Evan didn't respond, just licked his lips, staring ahead.

"I mean, you did get . . . *hurt*. Sure you wanna do this?"

After a shallow breath, Evan sat up, nodded. "Eh, let's just do it."

"Okay. Good then. For me, I mean, I can just shrug it off. It sucks, all that happened, but I made it out pretty lucky." Mark had both hands on the wheel, his grip tight. "To be honest, I don't wanna revisit this crap. I don't want to think about that psycho asshole who was never a friend of ours. Not really. Don't want to revert back to the puberty days when we were all losers—"

"Well, we're still losers."

Mark grinned, to which the little crow's feet around his

squinty eyes became more pronounced. "Okay, but still, don't want to go back. Homework, pop quizzes, waiting for the freakin' bell to ring. No, no. I'm busy. I got stuffs to do, can't even stay that long. There is only one single damn reason I'm here. One."

With a half-glance to the side, Evan shifted in place.

"To make sure you're all right."

Smirking, he reached over and clamped down on Mark's shoulder, gave it a good shake.

"Oh, and live vicariously through you since you're single."

9

THE TWO FRIENDS followed the bend in the parking lot to the entrance of the cultural center. A few steps up to sliding glass doors, then there was a reception table with pamphlets and sign-in sheets. Next to that was a big poster board with the mascot and the name of the school, as well as CLASS OF 2002 in big white letters, all capital, sans serif. Evan picked up a rectangular sticker that read HI MY NAME IS and placed it on the left side of his chest. Mark shook his head with a sigh, did the same after some hesitation. Both put fictional names of their favorite fictional characters, which they used to do when they went to comic book conventions.

Evan smirked. "Lookin' good, Peter."

As they entered into the main hall from the lobby, all the tables set up with clean fabric and fancy centerpieces came into view. Half the seats were filled and the other half started to fill up. There were the usual things expected at this sort of event, banquets or conferences or even a wedding: folded napkins, various silverware, candles and candies and mints.

"Funny. We used to ditch pep rallies and spirit assemblies, and now here we are, coming to this little get-together of our own accord."

"Hehe, true. So many other things I'd rather be doing right now."

Mark searched the tables, trying to pick out a good spot. Following close behind, Evan scanned the room. It was interesting seeing his old classmates again. Once upon a time, ages ago, he would strut down the hallways and clap palms, fist bump, high five, wave, smile, even hug some of these people. But all these years later, he had trouble even recognizing their faces.

I wonder if she's here . . .

"Uh, how 'bout this one? Not too packed, and we can see the stage and also who else is coming in."

"Sure, dude. That'll work."

There was someone staring from a nearby table, and Evan narrowed his eyes as he tried to remember. The man had a confident gaze with a slow nod. His wife returned with a small plate of fruits and cheeses, and two glasses of iced tea. It clicked then—it was the guy on the cart from the auditorium that day. The gangsta that was headed down a bad path. Evan heard he was doing good—got married, had kids, started a charity organization and was involved in his church. He smirked back, raised a hand up with a wave.

Imagine how many lives this person must have touched. Imagine how many lives the family and friends of this person must have touched. Would all that have happened if the attack at Washington never occurred?

Evan noticed security guards trying to appear inconspicuous but sticking out like sore thumbs along the outside perimeter. Mark had pointed out there was security outside the building earlier, too. It was obvious they were making their rounds. A couple of news vans were parked out front, not a producer and reporter but rather a small team for outside shots and footage, perhaps for a smaller segment to air.

Just then, he was tackled from behind. As Mark pulled the chair out, about to sit down, he paused and watched the exchange. Evan turned, leaning and pivoting on one foot.

"Michelle??? What the eff!?" He shoved at her. It was like they were in school again, where that behavior was acceptable and normal.

"How ya been, buddy."

"Come sit. It's been a hella long time."

She inclined her head, gazed across the large room over the crowd. "Oh, uh, I'm actually on the other side. Over there."

"Ah. Okay. Well, I been pretty good. Just moved a few months ago."

"Right, right. I saw online. You were over there a long time. How's it like being back on the island?"

Evan twisted the corner of his lips, nodded. "Still adjusting, I guess. But it's not too bad. Can't complain."

"I kind of bounce around, since my job. I was up and down the east coast for a while, then the south, and now the midwest. Like it there a lot."

"Cool, cool."

Michelle gazed across again, to where someone waved her over. "I better go check in with Erin. We'll catch up later, okay?"

He watched his old friend make her way back. She appeared just the way she used to be, with her crooked glasses and messy hair like she had been in a tornado. Put a camera around her neck hanging down from a thick strap and it would almost be indistinguishable.

When Michelle hugged her significant other in the distance, a thin girl with clear glasses and wavy bleached hair parted to one side, Evan smirked to himself.

About midway through the space, as his eyes shifted focus, Evan noticed another familiar someone. It was the short girl also in the auditorium that day. Of all the things he encountered, other than the showdown in the library, the events of the auditorium were still vivid and clear. Hard to forget such vindictive malice, that sick twisted game of feral cats and lab mice. Now, she stood there, laughing along, both arms wrapped around her husband's side.

Sigh.

Hey, at least there was some good.

Just then, the lights began to dim, a warning that the event would soon start. Evan felt a sinking sensation deep within his chest. He wasn't ready. He came to the opening of the rabbit hole, peered into it, but remained outside. In the now darkened space, the entrance which remained bright became clearer. While the rest of the crowd took their seats or made their way back to their tables, Evan stood in place gazing at the door, as if he was being compelled to.

Years of life can drag on. An entire decade can flash forward with the snap of a finger or the blink of an eye. This particular moment slowed until every passing second was a fraction of a second, of a microsecond . . .

He felt the corners of his eyes water, the hairs on his arms raise up. His bottom lip lowered as, in the faraway entrance, a radiant soul appeared to manifest. With a turn around the frame then a pause in the middle of it, the door became a full body portrait. She glanced to her left, panned over to her right, searching. Everyone else almost all seated but the two of them, their eyes met from opposite sides of the open space. At first, her eyes passed his, but with a quick mini-double take, again returned their mutual stare. It was an entire lifetime in a single instant. He licked his lips, swallowed a hard dry swallow. She nibbled at her bottom lip.

Jude . . .

Evan was astonished by her beauty, taken aback, nervous, smitten, at a loss for words. He was frozen in place. A part of him longed for her but another part was also hesitant, resistant.

That was when he felt a pat on his forearm, a yank on his sleeve. He watched as almost in sync, Judith was approached and hugged, led away from the perfectly lit and perfectly spaced full portrait to a different table in a different section, on the other side of the room.

Along the back wall, Max made his way towards Evan and Mark, with swift shoves at the wheel rims propelling him forward in a gliding motion. Mark reached over and slid one of the chairs away to make space.

"'Sup."

Max's usual low mumble had a little bit of a slur to it. His movements a touch unsteady, he rolled in next to them, pushed the brakes into place.

Evan smirked, leaned in. "Getting started a li'l early, huh?"

"Hey. School spirits, right?" Max reached in his inside pocket, jiggled a small silver flask then let out a sharp hyena laugh. "*Teen* spirits."

Mark shook his head, crossed his arms and slouched in place.

"All right, all right. Just take it easy." Evan said, watching him take in the moment, take in the crowd. "Love the ensemble, dude."

Max wore a gray turtleneck and a black blazer, almost a sarcastic take on how festive this was all supposed to be. Instead of a fedora hat, this time he had an Irish style flap cap. Evan had on a long sleeve collar shirt with a sleek necktie, and Mark a regular polo with an argyle pattern.

"Ah, look at us. The ol' gang back together." Mark reached both arms out, across the shoulder blades of Evan and of Max, grinning a wide grin that made his squinty eyes even squintier. "This is fuckin' horrible."

There was a slight squeak in the speaker system as the class president hovered over the podium mic. It was a generic welcome speech, with official announcements, a rundown of raffle tickets and the silent auction. She stepped aside as a video flickered on the projector screen behind her.

Despite technology having improved, the footage was grainy and lower quality. This was from before the transition to digital, actual film. A lot changed in that decade, as emphasized by the recording playing.

Vague flashes spewed from within the rabbit hole, like a vortex through time. The JROTC kids unfolding the flag and pulling the ropes to send it on up, sloppy salutes to match. The administration building. Buildings A through H, M-building, N-building. The long driveways running parallel. The portables. The cafeteria, gym, library. Sets of bleachers in the fields, on the track. Students walking in between classes, backpacks over one shoulder and textbooks in the crook of their arm. Students with their heads down working on different assignments. Teachers writing on the chalkboard, erasing, then writing again. Clapping along at the pep rally, at the spirit assembly. Doing jumping jacks. Shoving at one another, hugging, joking, laughing . . .

Between scenes, Evan glanced across at Judith. For a brief moment, Judith glanced back. He remembered the triangle and the tornado, fleeting emotions of adolescence that stayed pure in his memories. Now, perhaps that so-called triangle was broken, but the possibility of a tornado was still up in the air, pun intended.

More flashes. This time, the freshman and sophomore banquets, school dances, school plays and talent shows. Images from prom: kids in their tuxes and dresses, corsages and boutonnieres and hand bouquets, swaying on the dance floor. The tennis team and the judo team. Air riflery. School newspaper and school yearbook staff, a couple shots with Evan himself along with Michelle. Images from graduation: the procession, moving the tassel from one side to the other in unison, tossing their hats in the air.

And then, what they all dreaded. Clips from the news. Aerial views of the school with rising plumes of smoke. Police officers securing the campus, leading students out to safety. Medical staff assisting those injured and consoling those traumatized. Crying, wailing. Holding one another. Holding hands. Lit candles and flowers and cards scattered along the back fence, tied with bows. A huge crowd gathered in the street.

Little bumps formed on his skin. His face and teeth felt hollow then. His chest sank. He tilted his head and adjusted in place, closed his eyes then reopened them.

There were photos of those less fortunate. Kids he didn't know, some he had seen around, and others he had seen in passing. The girl with long hair and droopy eyes had her cheek in her palm with a half-smile, eyebrows furled. The kid in uniform with a stern and stoic look in his eye in a slight side profile faded in and out. More kids continued to glide by horizontally in a slow moving marquee, in memoriam.

If the girl with piercings attended, it would have been a small gathering of those who endured the horrors in the auditorium that day. The gangsta and the goth. The short girl. Evan. And the puppet and the jester. A big black duffel bag. All on the stage in the spotlight in front of the empty rows.

Mark covered his mouth as he let out an extended yawn, shuddering. Max took a deep breath then snuck in a subtle swig.

As the rest of the presentation wrapped up, Evan instead

turned his focus to the pamphlet on the table. He leafed through its contents, flipped to the back of it. The images, the blocks of text, the information and testimonials—it was all inauthentic to him. Some guy in some back room put it together, unknowing, unwitting. The truth was, being a Washington alum could not be put down in a small six-section folded glossy sheet. To know what happened that day. To know what it was like between those walls, under those ceilings. The smell and feel of each chalkboard and analog clock, each shelf with textbooks, each row and column of desks. And to have that whole universe, that little bubble, ripped to shreds when the first shots fired.

The class president announced more presentations after the break for dinner. She asked to be courteous and proceed in an orderly fashion.

Max rolled backward, pivoted, making his way toward the buffet with a small line growing. Mark stood in place, waited for Evan.

"Uh, h-hold on . . ." He snapped himself out of his little daydream. "D-do you wanna go say hey . . ."

"I seen her." Mark put his hand out on his shoulder, leaned in closer. "C'mon, let's go make this more awkward."

Each group of alumni started to gather in their respective cliques, like they were back on campus. The jocks and the cheerleaders were by one table, and the smart kids who all used to sit in the front of the class by another. Cool kids with their cool clothes and their cool shoes, cool hair—undoubtedly in their cool cars as well. The delinquents and the outsiders, this time, had the option to not participate. Still, there were a few.

During the speech and slideshow, it had been quiet, but now was a growing cacophony of noise and chatter. Some jumped up and down in excited voices as they hugged. Others laughed, bent forward and slapped their knees as they relived the glory days and simpler times.

As they passed from one side of the large room to the other, there were some waves, some nods, even a fist bump and a handshake. It was congested in certain areas, and they had to push and squeeze through. Evan peeked in between heads and necks and backs. Mark struggled to keep up, almost falling behind.

Like an empty rowboat making its way towards the distant shore, he drifted closer. He could see her and her one friend by the far wall, growing in size as they approached. Judith raised a hand to cover her mouth as she laughed, her deep dimples in her cheeks peeking through. The movement sent a slight sweep of her bangs across her brow.

She turned to face him and Mark as they joined in, the scene sending flashbacks of prom to his mind. Of course, reliving the prom and reliving the day of the shooting were very different things.

Mark passed him, bumbling forward. "Hey, Judy!"

He did a quick side hug to both girls, stepped away. Evan hugged her friend first and then Judith. The two embraced tight, both closing their eyes and breathing in deep and slow, a slight sway as they did. A whiff of her perfume shot through his nostrils and into his lungs, sending a small shiver down the small of his back to his tailbone.

It was a different scent, an intoxicating aroma, but it had the same effect as it did back then. Pausing all movement, altering reality, the fragrance touching him on a level deeper than in his metaphysical body.

When he stood back, Evan scanned her up and down. She wore a sleek dress with thin straps, just a touch of cleavage and leg showing. Her hair was an immaculate ombre that had a wave and a bounce professionally done.

"Jude . . ." Evan smirked to himself.

No longer mere memories in his subconscious or a collection of still images in cyberspace, there she was, right in front of him, almost more beautiful than he had remembered.

"You guys remember Huifang?"

Mark grinned. "Of course, how could I forget."

In the weeks leading up to prom, Mark didn't have a date and neither did Huifang. The four of them started to hang at the shopping center sometimes after Evan and Judith got together, so it seemed natural to pair the two. Except she hated his guts.

Judith smiled wide, turning the corners of her eyes up with a sparkle. "You seem the exact same, yet also different at the same time."

A quiet round of laughter between them all, standing together in an uneven rhombus shape.

"Heh. Got rid of that nineties hair, right?"

Leaning in, she tapped at his name tag. Her fingernails, like her hair, was pristine. "And why does this say Steve?"

"Back in college, me and Mark used to do that. Look at his."

She shook her head and rolled her eyes, in a teasing manner.

"Maybe, uh, let's go get some food 'fore they run out." Huifang fidgeted on her feet, almost not making eye contact.

They nodded in agreement, turned to re-enter the crowd. Evan peeped across, saw Max stacking his plate up high.

"Oh. Just so you know." Mark raised both hands as he followed along. It was Huifang, Mark, then Evan and Judith. "I'm already taken."

Huifang, much like that night at prom before, appeared annoyed. If it were still senior year, she would have hit him—once, and then once more for good measure. She rolled her eyes, shook her head, but continued on. Mark glanced back, a grin across his face.

As the groups of alums started to settle, there was enough room that Evan waited for Judith and the two walked together side by side. Images from the old lab, the study room, the fields, lying in the grass, sitting on the swings, feeding ducks all entered his mind. He licked his lips while facing down to the carpet.

No doubt the campus had changed by now. The laboratories in the back of the science classes were redone. The library was renovated, with all new computers and all new computer systems. The fields now had a memorial site built in between the stream and the back fence. Even the nearby park had improvements to the gazebo, playground, swings and the grass and the astroturf.

"I'm glad I came."

He wasn't used to hearing her voice again. Kind of like her perfume, the sound of it sent a ripple effect through the surrounding matter, including the very cells in his body.

"Me too. I, uh, wasn't sure how I would feel about all of this."

He turned left then right, gazing at all occurring around them.

"Of course, I wanted to see you . . ."

Not sure why those words slipped out from his lips, he regretted blurting out such a thing, lowered his head.

"Same. I . . ." Judith faced him, her lips thinned, a touch of pink showing in her cheeks. "It's been too long."

With that, the regret melted away, as did a piece of himself. Their hands grazed between them, his pinky finger to her index finger. He felt that familiar electrical charge, took a deep breath while it washed over each of his senses.

Do I . . .

Do I still . . .

Evan cleared his throat. "W-where's your fiancé? I figured he'd be here."

"Oh, he couldn't make it, actually. Last second thing. Super busy."

To this, he squinted and furled his brow, scrunched his lips a bit, almost unable to believe the chances of that.

"Good. I didn't wanna meet the bastard anyway." Evan said it as an innocent joke, though there was a tiny accompanying sting.

Judith smiled, with a soft laugh.

"Being medical director is a big, important job, huh."

She nodded. "Yeah. I mean, I barely get to see him. I'm busy too, but I do want to have a life. You know? Life's too short."

"How you like it? Being a doctor in the ER. Like, you're doing it. Helping people, making a difference. What you always wanted. What you always worked towards."

They stood in the moving line. Mark chatted with Hui-fang, niceties and platitudes that filled the silence, enough that Evan and Judith had a quiet moment.

"I don't think about it too much. But you're right, even back then, with my mom and my dad pushing me, and then everything that happened." She took a deep breath, crinkled her brow. "It's nice. I mean, it is hard, yes, but I feel 'whole' doing it. You know? Where I don't mind putting on scrubs every day, fighting traffic both ways, putting on the name badge, getting busy and dirty and stressed out . . . Like a sorta calling, I guess."

Evan shifted, faced up. "Proud of you, Jude."

He reached for an empty plate, handed it over. She took it, grabbing a paper napkin, stepping close as they lined up along the buffet.

"And how 'bout you? Where's your girlfriend? What about your work?"

"I actually, uh, am single right now. We broke up a little while ago."

She nudged him at the elbow, nibbling her bottom lip. "I knew. Like you, kind of almost glad. Didn't wanna see that bitch anyway."

They both laughed, started to fill their plates. He added a small scoop of rice. She took some salad, drizzled some vinaigrette, placed down a piece of bread. Each took a sideways step.

"I'm only kidding, of course. You okay?"

"Yeah, just . . . doin' my thing." He used tongs to grab some chicken strips, a couple slices of braised beef. "As for job, I'm an administrative assistant. At a real estate firm. Pretty lame."

"Really? That's kind of weird to me, imagining you in some stuffy desk job in some cramped office. Never would've thought."

She's right.

I've become this cog in the machine, a shill.

"Nah, you got a point. I'll be honest, I kind of hate my fucking job. I hate going in there. Hate answering phones, entering info in the damn database, clocking in and out for lunch. I kind of hate the whole 'corporate' atmosphere. Bullshit meetings all the time, bullshit e-mails. Everyone is so full of crap."

Judith giggled, nodded along.

"We got some of that too. So much red tape, y'know? Almost bureaucratic all the time. Do you see yourself staying there long?"

"No way. I'm working on a li'l something, keeping it under wraps for right now. Think I just kinda need to do my own thing. Go another way."

She stared ahead, pondered for a moment.

"Maybe . . . Maybe you should. You're kind of a free spirit."

"Yeah. Totally."

He never heard that before, and it kind of struck a chord. Something clicked in his head, as he stepped sideways to the left.

Mark's plate started to get pretty full, but he was determined to fit even more. He tiptoed while balancing the growing pile of food. Huifang stared with a blank expression.

They returned to their spot by the far wall. Mark borrowed the last empty chair, next to Huifang who sat back down. Evan hovered with his plate in his hand near Judith.

"You don't wanna sit?" She glanced up.

"Nah, I'm okay. Just here for the company, and the view."

Each exchanged a quick lingering stare then took little bites. She scooted over, leaving enough room that they both could sit.

He shook his head but obliged. "Just like in high school, huh."

It was strange being near her again, their thighs now pressed together. It was strange being near all these people. Life unravels in its own mysterious way, he concluded. Kindred souls become entangled and star-crossed for a season, for a reason, then unwind in different directions, collide under circumstance, change trajectory.

For a moment, he envisioned this multiverse, and a possible timeline in which they were still together and different things happened. They were happy, in love, and had the three kids and the three dogs they used to talk about, in a nice house, in the nice area of town. Evan shook the thought away, smirking to himself, sighing to himself. He admired the curvature of her cheek and the slender of her collar bone, the sheen of her hair . . .

I'll savor this, one last time.

For a single night.

And then I'll let you go . . . Again.

The night would go on like that. Sitting then standing together, walking together. With an occasional graze or flirtatious gesture, the occasional lock of their eyes that spoke more than words ever could. Evan and Judith caught up with old classmates, laughed, joked, pretended like nothing but good things happened back then. They stayed close, and it was unclear whether it was out of habit or out of pure desire to, after all these years.

At one point, Mark regaled old tales of how they used to run around and cause mischief with exaggerated movements of his hands. Huifang shook her head, but smiled. Judith covered her mouth with her palm, tilted in towards Evan, shoving him with a light push. Michelle and Erin later blended in, making their rhombus shape a hexagon. The two laughed along with the rest. When Max made his way over, that hexagon became a heptagon. He let out his loud hyena laugh, slapping down on the armrest. It was turning out to be quite the joyous occasion—until the overhead lights cut out, and the far windows shattered in one by one.

10

It was a subtle build, the gathering, the presentation, dining and drinks, then the mingling, which had gone from low voices to loud voices. Awkward at first, but before long, it felt natural, like nothing had changed. Same dirty jokes. Same swear words. Same shoving and hugging and leaning on shoulders. Those good friends from way back were still good friends, even though some may have moved, may have lost touch, may have forgotten how much these familiar people meant. It appeared like slow motion to him, like a montage. Evan consoled Judith with a side hug, after the gang teased her. Huifang appeared to enjoy herself now. Mark patted Max on the shoulder. Michelle turned whatever topic into something raunchy, to which Erin raised her hands up, disapproving and disassociating. With all this, of course, a mundane thing such as the sound of screeching tires almost went unnoticed.

"Did . . . Did you guys hear . . ." Max turned backward, glanced over. "The fuck was that?"

Evan blinked to himself. He also heard it but figured it was nothing. One, he didn't want to ruin the moment. Two, car crashes happened all the time. Back in high school, living at home with his mom and dad and little brother, there was a busy road right out in front of their cheap apartment on the ground floor. He pretty much heard one every single day. And so, the distant and faint screeching then banging of mangled metal against muffled conversation and laughter didn't quite phase him.

"Eh. Prob'ly nothing."

He faced to where Max peeped, dismissed it, then returned to the group.

"Don't even worry about it."

One by one, Evan gazed into the faces of his peers. They were all getting older, changing into evolved versions of themselves. Mark, he had known forever, and would probably know for forever more, even if the few times they saw each other was for their birthdays as life kept them both preoccupied. This new Max was far from perfect, but in certain ways, he was somehow better than he once was. Michelle was doing well: good job with good pay, got to travel, was a foodie. And Judith seemed to be just fine. They each grew up, each settled down, had found their own place and their own pathway.

"Hey." Judith leaned in. "What ever happened to Filbert?"

"Filbert . . . the fish?"

"Haha, yeah. You remember, right?"

He swallowed a dry swallow, licked his lips, as he glanced in her eyes. There was a time when those almond eyes belonged to him. Back when he would run across town just to see her, battered flowers in hand. Back when he would lie down and talk with her on the phone for hours—about nothing, about everything. Back when they were just learning about love and relationships, how to kiss, how to touch, exploring their bodies like unknown wonderlands.

"I'm pretty sure he died."

Both bawled from laughter, their bodies shuddering in unison.

Unbeknownst to them, the faint screeching tires now became quiet footsteps in the outside hallway, inching closer and closer.

Judith seemed to linger, her almond eyes staring right into his, right through him, as she pushed her bangs aside and tucked her hair behind her left ear. He hadn't seen her do that in a long time, and forgot how enchanting it was.

"Evan, can we—"

The lights above them shut off. First, the front end by the buffet, then the middle by the stage, and then the far side where they were all standing. It went from bright to dim, to halfway dark, then pitch black.

What in the hell!?

All the attendees remained in place, confused, some turning to each other and shrugging, others trying to peep over the crowd. Their heptagon followed right along, with muted whispers, raising their hands up and darting their heads left and right. Mark flinched, almost did a double take. Michelle squinted and furled her brow.

"Uh . . ."

"You've got to be kidding me."

Glass shattered, a sharp cracking noise causing those nearby to gasp and scream. The crowd stood frozen, certain alums glancing over. Then another window broke, then another. Those sounds pierced through the air, sending a shockwave of panic and an eruption of chaos.

Holy fuckin' shit!

With the terror unfolding around them, it all came rushing back—the bullet holes, the bullet casings, bloody footprints, pools of blood. The horror. The pain. The questions. The trauma. Scared, that they might not graduate. Scared, that they might not lose their virginity. Why was this happening? How could this happen to them, again?

The security guards yelled to remain calm, to get down, but of course nobody listened. Instead, all at once, they shoved and clawed, thrashed about like fish in a shrinking barrel.

Michelle and Erin disappeared in the sea of bodies, as did Huifang. Ducking, crouching, Mark put both hands on his head. Evan reached across her far shoulder, pulled Judith close to him. Max slouched down the back of his chair, shuddering in place.

"No!!! Oh my God!"

"Jesus Christ. What do we do?"

Evan faced ahead with his jaw dropped, breathing in slow and deep. He looked Max straight in the eye, shifted towards Mark. When he turned and saw Judith with both hands clasped in a pleading motion, he went blank . . .

On the day of the shooting, they were all unprepared: students, teachers, faculty, staff. It was one of the first of its kind. After that, regular lockdown drills were instituted. However, in the moment, still—like now, at their little reunion—under extreme and dire conditions, there is no way to remain calm. No way to remember a silly acronym. Can't wait for law enforcement. Can't hope things will be all right. It is a simple matter of life and death. Fight or flight or freeze.

A clinking noise sounded from the shattered windows. Something metallic dropped on the ground, rolled, then hissed. A plume of smoke rose from the ground, sending more screams and yelling and cries, another surge of movement through the mob of bodies scattering. Another clink. Another hiss.

With this, Evan moved his arm from her shoulder, instead held her hand tight, interlocking their fingers.

"Don't. Let. Go."

Judith nodded, sniffled. Her eyes widened.

"E-Evan?" Mark watched the two clouds waft and spread. "What's the plan?"

He darted his head, searched around the room. There was an exit door sign illuminated but a huge crowd gathered in front of it, either locked or backed up.

Max crouched low, listening. He hyperventilated. His fingers trembled.

"I see some windows back that way. I say we bust 'em in, make our way out." Evan now had a serious glare. "We can't stay here."

"Should we wait for the police?"

"Fuck the police!"

Bang. Bang, bang.

There were shots in the hallway by the entrance. Security guards yelled to freeze, drop the gun.

Bang. Bang.

A dull hard thud of someone hitting the ground in the exchange of gunfire. Each shot sent flashes through the broken windows and thick smoke.

Come on, we gotta go.

Hurry up.

Shit. Shit. Shit.

Evan led their small parade through the riotous frenzy. He grabbed an unused steak knife from the table. He held it blade down in one hand, clasping Judith's hand in the other. It reminded him of the butterfly knife. Drips of nervous sweat gathered on his forehead.

Some people tripped over each other in front of him, attempting to flee in opposite directions. Others flipped tables and chairs over to make way. Others hid beneath the table.

Mark grabbed an empty metal tray, held it in front of his torso like a shield. Max peeped back over his shoulder, keeping pace. Security guards again tried to yell to remain calm, to yell instructions, pointing which way to go, but to no avail.

Bang, bang. Bang.

"Here! This way!"

Bang.

There was another dull hard thud in the far hallway.

At first, Evan rammed into the glass with his shoulder but the window remained intact. It was narrow but tall, sturdy. Mark tried using the metal tray but it just left a nick. Evan grabbed a nearby chair and hit it with the legs, making a tiny crack. *Come on!!!* He repositioned the chair in his hands, hitting it with the back, widening the crack. He stepped to get some movement and a little bit of swing before smashing it open. *Finally!* Mark broke the rest of the shards off with the tray, keeping his face back. Judith laid down cloth napkins over the bottom.

"Okay. Jude, you first."

Evan helped her up and over to the other side.

"Mark . . ."

He stood by, watched as Mark crawled in next.

Evan then turned to Max, but Max already rolled backward in the crowd. "Hey, wait! Where are you—"

"I can't fit through that tiny window!"

Damn it.

He glanced at the smashed window, did a quick calculation in his head. He sighed and shook his head. There were a few of these windows around the space, for decorative purposes, none of which could fit the wheelchair. Evan turned to go after Max.

"No, no! Evan, you crazy?" Mark waved his hands, motioned for him to follow them in. "Get over here."

"But M-Max, I—"

"Evan." Judith stared at him with pleading eyes, a single tear about to roll down her cheek. "Not this time. Please."

She reached through, held out an open palm. From that angle, the ring on her finger gleamed. There was an ache in the pit of his stomach, to which he closed his eyes and paused. After a second of hesitation, he reluctantly grabbed her hand, stumbled through the window and joined them.

You better be careful.

Don't do anything stupid, Max.

Evan squeezed her hand as they ran down the long and open hallway. The ballroom was in the middle of the building, surrounded by a series of corridors. Sharp turns followed more sharp turns like a maze. There were a few doors lined in a row. They jiggled the handles of each one but they were all locked. It was another long hall then another. A line of doors once more but their hopes began to sink as each jiggle amounted to nothing. *God damn!* He could feel it then, that this was taking too long. Did they maybe go the wrong way? Was this a dead end? Was there no way out?

Keeping pace at their side, Mark started to take the lead but all of a sudden skidded on his feet. A clink and a hiss came from around the corner, causing them to stop in place, and a cloud of gray smoke sprayed up into the air from the floor like a rogue wave.

"Oh! Shit!!!"

"Nooo."

Through the smoke, they could see a silhouetted figure. There was something in its hands. Against the wavy plumes, the silhouette warped and stretched like in the reflections of a funhouse mirror. Evan sensed a sinister nature in the entity unraveling beneath the haze—sensed malice, sensed a lack of humanity. On its face were two round glass circles and a rubber strap. The shape of a metallic object in both hands hovered, slow, protruding forward, pointed straight at the three as they staggered backwards.

In adult life, the passing of time is so rapid. It is rainwater gushing via tiny waterfalls after a heavy thunderstorm. Forks in the road lead to wide ponds, lead to fallen trees, burnt bridges, and moss covered rocky formations. A moment such as this one, it is so apparent that time can speed up as much as it slows down. It pauses altogether, even. Time is dynamic . . . Time is fluid . . .

Evan shut his eyes, winced, fearing the worst.

Bang.

One of them flew back, jerked in a twisting motion at the shoulder. When their arm and their leg involuntarily flailed out, they all tripped together onto the tile floor like dominos lined. The sound of their bodies thudding received a dull echo that bounced off of the walls and ceiling.

"Jude! Jude!?"

Please God no.

He turned over on his stomach, lifted his head with his jaw dropped. She sat up, stared back across, her eyes narrowed as she gasped. Facedown, writhing in pain and grunting, they each watched as the unthinkable occurred.

"MARK!!!!!"

Evan slid on the floor to where his friend trembled on all fours. He put a hand on the back of his shoulder blade.

Step.

Step, step.

From behind, the silhouette now manifested in clear and vivid form. Dressed all in black, combat boots on, a hunting knife in a sheath at the ankle, curly hair, goggles, with a camouflage vest—the rifle was still raised, now to the side, ready to take the next shot.

No! No!!!

Nooo!

Evan leapt in front of Judith with both arms out, glared, bit down. He knelt on one knee while she curled in a ball behind him. Judith tugged at the hem of his shirt, whimpering.

The quiet stillness was drowned out in loud shouts back and forth. On either side of them, armed guards rushed forward with weapons drawn. The shooter turned, pulling the trigger, disappearing into the fog. Flashes of gunfire lit up the hallway.

Bang, bang.

Bang, bang, bang.

One of the guards asked if they could move, told them to get out of there if they were able, then pursued the shooter. Evan and Judith both nodded then faced Mark.

Bang.

"I-is he—?"

Again, Evan reached out to Mark, placing one hand over the back of his shoulder blade. He blinked to himself as he held his breath behind gritted teeth.

"Ugh . . . Fuuuck . . ." Mark dropped the metal tray on the floor with a clang. An indenture appeared like a bolt had been pushed through at the upper left corner. "Hurts so freaking bad, dude. Dammit . . ."

"Oh, thank God. Son of a bitch, what are the freaking chances."

It was a stroke of dumb luck that he happened to find that empty tray, happened to hold onto it, happened to hold it in just the right way at just the right time. That the thing was thick enough. That the shooter was far enough.

"Come on. We gotta go."

Evan started to help him up, but Mark winced and hissed to the touch. When he pulled the collar over, Evan saw the discoloration beneath his collar bone. A major bruise, deep purple.

"Jude."

He handed her the steak knife. She held it with both hands, nodded, faced down the hallway.

"Okay. Do you . . . Do you think you can do this . . . ?"

Mark didn't say anything, took a deep breath in and out, trying to psyche himself up. "AHHH!"

Together, they stumbled to their feet, following Judith who already started walking through the hallway. It was fuzzy gray like static, the haze thickening. Mark put his good arm around Evan at the shoulder. Evan held at his wrist, supporting the arm, and at the far hip, supporting the torso.

"It hurts, dude."

"I know. I know." Evan searched the tile floor where his own feet faded in the smoke. "We have got to get outta here, right now."

Mark grunted and moaned with each short step, a steady grimace across his usual grinning face.

"Aw, man. I—"

"You can do this. You have to do this."

"Fuuuck!"

"Come on, Markie Mark. Let's go."

Judith crept forward, holding the knife out in front of her. She stepped with caution, though it seemed the danger was behind them.

Bang. Bang.

In the distant hallway, around the corner, echoed gunshots continued along with muffled yells, then the sound of shuffling and reloading.

Bang.

"This way . . ." She feigned courage, began to step a little faster. "I see something up ahead . . . Maybe . . . Yeah!"

As she broke into a light jog, she disappeared from their view. They could hear her footsteps, and what sounded like a spring or a latch.

"Here!!! Hurry!"

When they got to the end of the hall, she held open one side of the double doors, let them pass through first. Mark broke free, hobbled down the stairs.

"You sure? Mark—"

"I'm good. Good enough anyway." He took his car keys out with one hand, held it over the front of his left shoulder, grunted as he stepped. "Let's get out of here!"

Evan turned to Judith, placed his hand on the small of her back. "How 'bout you? Jude, you okay?"

She nodded, tossed the knife in the bushes, followed.

Now, the air was clear again so Evan could see. Groups of alumni ran down the sidewalks and across the grassy hills. Cars jammed up at one entrance, honking, some screeching over the curb to freedom. A pair of patrol cars arrived, lining up next to others already parked, their red and blue lights flashing intermittently.

He almost tripped while scanning to the side, but Judith caught him. She held him at the chest, as they exchanged a quick glance.

Mark slowed, shifted side to side. "Fuck. I hope this is right."

"Yeah. We parked by that furniture place. 'Member?"

"Ugh!!!" Mark pulled forward, hissed, moaned. "Ah!"

Evan took the lead, held Judith close, as Mark prepped the

car keys with a solid jingle. They got in the back seat through the same passenger door as Mark hobbled into the driver's seat.

"You got this? You can drive?"

"It hurts like a bitch, but yeah. Let's go."

11

OFF TO ONE side, huddled together, Evan held Judith. He touched the line of his jaw to the side of her head as she sniffled, shuddered. The scent of her hair sent a small shiver throughout his body. He closed his eyes, breathed it in. His hand rubbed at her far shoulder. With a swift turn, Judith leaned back harder onto his collar bone. For a moment, despite change, despite feelings of disorientation and discombobulation, despite chaos, there was also calm and peace and a quiet stillness. All of the planets and stars and moons seemed to pause, freezing the world on its tilted axis. Evan remembered this . . . Remembered this feeling, this spark . . . That spark he would often ruminate on, dwell on, compare to, calculate. This pure glowing ember had been buried away for so long. A forgotten relic that now shined in his hands like sacred treasure uncovered. How could it be that after all this time, somehow, the one that got away, the one that slipped through his fingers, was in his arms once again?

Her legs were smooth, skin like porcelain, and the hem of her dress rode up as she tucked her knees up onto the cushion. His eyes wandered from the frills and wrinkles in her dress to where he could see down the chest area, where her bosoms rose and fell with each soft breath.

Forcing himself to face away, he instead faced out the window to the streets whizzing by in a slight blur.

What the hell just happened . . .

God. What's going on?

I hope Max is okay, Michelle, everyone else.

She nuzzled into him, pulled him tight. He reached up into her hair, stroked it, played with it, almost out of sheer habit. A ten-year-old habit come back in an instant.

You're just scared. That's all.

This is nothing.

Evan could feel Mark's eyes peek from the rearview mirror for a quick second, then return to the road ahead. He was careful rotating the wheel with one palm.

Many mixed emotions ran through Evan's mind. His heart raced, from both adrenaline and panic, but at the same time it also skipped a beat. Then it seemed to melt as old feelings floated to the surface—the sudden realization of how much he missed her, the degree to how bad he wanted her. Wanted to kiss her, to touch her, to ravage her.

They continued through the city streets a safe distance away, then pulled into the parking lot of a convenience store with bright fluorescent lights. Before stepping out, each took a moment to just breathe, just think and feel.

"Everybody doing okay?"

"Yeah, I think so. Gonna go get some ice."

Mark did seem a little better, far from fine, but better. Evan glanced down at Judith who leaned back, exhaled and nodded.

"Let's get water or whatever. Gather our composure. And we can all talk, plan, figure things out."

Mark put his hand on the handle, opened it, paused, then staggered up with a light grunt.

The two stayed in the back seat a little longer. After a while, they disconnected, unraveled, slinked away into two separate entities once again. When they both got out, he touched at her wrist, to which she turned around, pulled him in for a soft embrace.

It's okay. I'm glad you're okay.

Glad we're both here right now.

Judith let out one last sniffle, cleared her throat, gazed with her almond eyes that were now somber. She mouthed the words, thank you, and shifted.

He smirked as she walked ahead then held the door open.

Right by the counter, Evan saw a single packet of Extra Strength Tylenol hanging on the shelf. He waved it over the aisles. "'Ey. They got painkillers."

"Prolly cost an arm and a leg. But yeah, sure."

Mark came over with a bottle of soda, a cup of ice and a wad of napkins. Evan handed the pills to him as he went to the register, paid then went outside.

"Are you getting anything? A snack?"

"I'm not really hungry." She let out a nervous laugh, shook her head. "I could use a drink. And I don't even really drink."

Evan chuckled at the thought.

Mark leaned on the fender of the car, pressed the napkins full of ice against his shoulder and chest area. He groaned to himself in relief.

"Better?"

"Hell yeah."

She popped open her can of coconut water, took a slow sip. He twisted the cap of his enhanced sports drink but just held it.

"You gonna be all right? Should we go to the hospital?"

"I'll keep an eye, head down in the morning or somethin' if I need."

He put one arm out, rested his hand on his shoulder. "You're so lucky, dude. Got an angel looking over you."

An awkward pause in the night air. No breeze. Not a sound. Mark swallowed the pills with a good swig.

Evan took a belated sip, cleared his throat. "So, uh, what the hell happened back there? And what do we do now?"

"I mean, are we supposed to call 9-1-1?"

"Yeah. We will."

Judith folded her arms. "What was that? Who . . . ?"

"I have no idea." Evan shook his head, turned over to Mark.

"Maybe an old classmate?"

"Hmm. I have a feeling, no. Didn't recognize."

Shaking her head, facing down, Judith shuffled on her feet. "This is so weird. Part of me is so happy 'cause I haven't seen you guys in so long. But I also can't believe this."

"I know."

"Like, I'm back to that place. Scared. Confused. All that back there, it reminds me of being trapped in the cafeteria."

Evan put one arm around her.

"Yeah, this is kinda like when me and Jared were hiding out too. A little older now, but still too young to die." Mark blinked then arched his neck. "That bastard. I'm gonna kick his ass for missing out on all this fun."

Just then, a light buzz sounded from Evan's pocket. He reached down, took out his smartphone to check.

"It's Max. He's all right." He read the text aloud to everyone. "I must've missed it but Michelle is okay too."

Mark adjusted the napkins that were starting to soak

through, pressed it beneath the collar of his shirt now wet. He nodded along.

"That's good. Good. Great to hear."

"Uh . . ."

"What is it?"

Evan lowered the phone, half-tilted away. "Max says we should all meet up."

"I'm supposed to work early, catch up on paperwork. But y'know, under the circumstances, I ain't doing shit."

"Maybe you get that drink after all?"

Judith smiled. "I'll ask Huifang too. She might need it."

"Cool. I'll invite Michelle. The *real* reunion."

12

It was crowded and rowdy in the parking lot outside the club, with a small line gathered in front. The beat and the bass reverberated through the night air. Women in tight dresses clutched at their small purses, walked together in pairs of two or three. Some men overdressed, had too much jewelry or too much cologne. Some men creeped by the corner or the back wall, shady, sketchy. As security guards let guests in, they waved metal detector wands over them and checked the inside of their pockets. It was as if no one had heard about what happened: the gunfire, the smoke grenades, the panic, the pure pandemonium. Perhaps not. Perhaps they did and did not care. Michelle stood with Erin off to one side, talking amongst themselves, while Max talked to one of the workers by the service entrance.

Evan walked next to Judith, close together. Mark dragged a little behind, still in some pain. As they joined, they all hugged one by one, to which Mark winced to the touch. Max came over too, rolled up to them with a slight skid. Judith leaned over him, hugged him from the side while Evan clapped him on the arm.

"So glad to see your face, dude. Had us worried."

"I'm sorry we got separated."

Max raised a hand up, jutted his lower lip. "All good."

"Trust me. Not much better the route we went." Mark let out his usual wide shit-eating grin, perhaps a sign his pain was subsiding and he was almost back to normal.

"Uh. I know one of the bartenders so I got everybody's cover take care of . . ." Max said. "Ready to go?"

"We're still waiting for Jude's friend. But also, we should talk first, get it all out of our system."

"Yeah." Michelle shook her head, blinking to herself. "You okay? You got *hit?* You guys ran into the actual shooter???"

Judith faced down, took in a light breath.

"I came this close. Like, my pathetic little life flashed before my freaking eyes. Sure I'll need many, many years of psychotherapy. But I'm alive."

He pulled the collar of his polo shirt down, showed them the darkened area.

"That is one helluva nasty bruise." Erin stepped back from the sight of it. "Holy crap."

Max leaned in, examined with curiosity. "Damn."

"I'm still in shock."

"Same here. It brings flashbacks from being locked in the gym. I feel, like, PTSD or something." Michelle shook her head, folded her arms. "Afraid I might have a panic attack and break down at any moment."

"What was that, though?"

"I don't know." Evan now wore a serious glare, licked his lips. "All I saw were the smoke bombs, and some gun. The guy had on a vest and, like, goggles."

"Probably know more tomorrow. At least they caught him already."

Judith's eyes widened. "They did?"

"You guys don't get the alerts? I have the local news app." Michelle took out her phone. "It was pretty quick. Shots fired on both sides, and they managed to subdue the guy."

"Oh, good. 'Cause way too often cops tend to take their sweet-ass time or botch things up in these instances."

"Must be the reason they got armed security . . ."

"Speaking of cops, I did call. They're aware of the situation." Max tapped his finger on the wheel. "Priority now is evacuation, safety, medical assistance. All attendees will get a call for official statements, guessing sometime tomorrow. Some of us might have to go in, depending."

"Ah. Gotcha."

Judith glanced at each of them. "Feels like it wasn't even that long ago since the last shooting."

"Seriously."

They all grew quiet, reflected on the sad state of the world. How integral it was to their generation, to their graduating class.

It felt like nowhere was safe anymore. This kind of thing happened at high schools, even elementary schools. More than just schools and colleges, it happened in many different settings now. From nightclubs like the one behind them to movie theaters to music festivals, to churches, to the subway, to the grocery store. It was something of a phenomenon—a complicated issue with multiple implications on multiple levels. Nobody wanted to bring it up, nobody wanted to discuss it. Any kind of possible answer or solution appeared to be volatile or divisive to the general public. And so, it just continued on, like a bloodied stampeding elephant in the proverbial room . . .

Michelle checked her phone again. "Sounds like no one was injured. 'Cept this weirdo, of course. Few guards got hurt, but not alumni."

"Ugh. My fucking luck."

There was a round of laughter, perhaps an inappropriate amount.

"Should we even be out here? Like, talking, joking. I sort of feel bad." Judith folded her arms.

"Well, when's the next time we'll all be together? You know?" Evan turned to her, forced a smirk. "And also, what's done is done. You heard it. That psychopath is taken care of. And police said they'll be in touch."

"I say, a little alcohol wouldn't hurt." Max stretched his neck from side to side. "A lotta alcohol would be great."

"Ugh. I don't even drink."

"Just get you a girly drink, Mark." Evan shoved at him, and Mark shoved him back. "The girliest drink."

From the other side of the parking lot, Huifang made her way. As they came together again, they formed that same polygonal shape from the venue. Evan stood with Mark to his right, Judith to his left. As Huifang came closer, they could see that she dressed for the occasion, appeared quite stunning and provocative.

Mark grew pale in the face with his jaw hanging.

"Uh, you okay? You need to talk?"

"Nah. I just wanna forget all that, have some fun. I want to end this night on a good note."

"Well said. All righty then. Let's go."

It was dark, loud, but Evan could see and hear once his senses acclimated. The large interior had high ceilings, was wide open. A staircase winded up to the second floor with a private lounge. There were booths and tables around the exterior, a long counter in the middle, and of course the bar and kitchen at the far end. Max found a spot opposite side of the dance floor, and led them through the crowded space. They each sat down on the soft cushy couches set at an angle with a couple scattered seats around a glass table. Mark plopped on one of the chairs, next to Max who rolled backward, locking into place. Michelle and Erin took one of the couches while Evan, Judith and Huifang took the other.

"This spot okay?"

"Perfect. Good job, Max the Axe."

His awkward smile stretched wide whenever Evan used that nickname. Not sure where it came from. Just slipped out one day and it clicked. It would go on to become his username and alternate persona.

Evan turned from Max to Michelle, watched as she laughed so hard her shoulders shuddered up and down. Mark shook his head in faux disapproval, arms crossed, with a mixture of glare and grin. Judith and Huifang whispered into one another's ears right next to him.

He sighed to himself with a small smirk, glanced over at the dance floor where bodies bumped and grinded.

Oval shaped, the area had sets of steps going down from three sides, and one long ramp. It was lower than the rest of the interior, kind of like a pit. The DJ booth was up top, with two big neon speakers blaring by the laptop and turntables. Metal rafters lined the perimeter with stage lights and lasers pointed down in multicolored diagonals. Every now and then, an occasional blast of fog floated over the surface of the lino-leum, to which the crowd roared and cheered.

"What's everybody drinking? I'll get the first round." Max's mumble was somehow always audible in these settings. He must have gotten used to it over the years.

"Uh . . ." Mark rubbed his chin, scratched his head.

"I'll get a beer."

"Me too."

Evan leaned in, shouted through the noise. "You know me. Vodka tonic."

"You usually get gin tonic first. Ha."

"Hey, let's get right into it."

"That's the plan." Max pounded the rim of the wheel. "So, beer, beer, vodka. Ladies?"

"A . . . margarita?"

"No, no. How 'bout two mojitos."

"Cool. Mark, I'm getting your ass a mai tai."

"Wait. That's not too strong, right?"

"Nah."

Evan smirked.

Mark pulled his phone out of his pocket, started texting away, no doubt updating the future wife his location and whereabouts, let her know he was alive.

"Need us to go with you?"

"I think . . ." Max turned around, peering into the crowd. "Ah, yeah, they come to the table too. Sometimes, anyway."

He waved to the waitress, put in the long order. There were some extra instructions in there as well, to which Michelle again laughed. As the waitress bent over right by Mark's face, her short shorts rode up to her butt. Judith and Huifang giggled.

The friend reached behind, past Judith, tugged on Evan's sleeve. "Hey. We all better dance later. Okay? I need to dance."

Evan smirked. "We'll dance our asses off."

Huifang smiled, let go.

"What is this?" Judith held her arm up, the inside of her wrist showing an inked stamp.

He lifted his next to hers, their forearms and fingers

grazing with a slight touch, like an electrical charge. Evan unknowingly held his breath.

"I-I can't tell either."

Not sure if thought or logic escaped him, or he just wanted to keep talking, keep their arms suspended in mid-air side by side.

"Lemme see." She pressed further against him, gazing at the two stamps.

Evan couldn't help but squirm in place. Their skin touching, their thighs and bodies huddled together in the dark, the fragrance of her perfume. It was all so intoxicating. He leaned in closer.

Should we be out here? Tonight, like this?
With what happened earlier?
And she's engaged . . .
Playing with fire. I gotta be careful.

The waitress came back with a tray and a pitcher. She put down the pitcher first, which was full of ice. There were three bottles and four glasses.

"Mark, ice cubes for you."

"Sweet. Thanks."

Michelle and Erin held their bottles up, waited for the others. Max did the same. Judith and Huifang took their drinks, stirred the mint leaves. Evan waited for Mark, his hand over the top of the glass with the thin straw between his fingers. Mark was hesitant, reluctant, but gave in and took the drink as well.

Each of them in their radical heptagon shape around the glass table hovered their drinks together.

"To Wash and back, twice now." Evan turned to them one by one. "And, as always, forever, to those that weren't so lucky."

"Cheers."

"Here, here."

"Kampai!"

The glasses and bottles all clinked together, some with a faint splash almost spilling over.

Evan took a swig then licked his lips.

Judith sipped, smiled. She turned to Huifang, told her it was pretty good.

"AHHH!" Mark gasped for air as if he had been held underwater. "Tastes like burning!!!"

Michelle slapped her knee, keeled over to one side, bawling. The others laughed along, teased. Mark stuck out his tongue and gagged.

"Guess Max's friend hooked it up, huh." Evan stretched one arm out, patting him on the shoulder.

"Just wait 'til you get the AMF." Max snickered.

"What the hell's an AMF?"

Before the group even recovered from that initial cheers and round of heckling, the waitress bent over again, placing down shot glasses and mixed glasses of juice and soda from the tray.

"Max. What'd you do?"

"Tequila shots, mofos."

Mark shook his head and muttered under his breath, in annoyed acceptance of his fate. Michelle and Erin knew what to do and led the group, Max right along with them.

"Uh, Evan. I don't get it." Judith shook her head.

"Haha. This is a chaser, to help kill the aftertaste. Juice is prob'ly better."

"Okay. And this?" She turned to him again, eyebrows raised.

"That's salt and lime. First, the salt, then drink, then the lime. 'Lick, shoot, suck.' Got it?"

"Um, all right . . . 'Lick, shoot, suck' . . ." She laughed to herself. "Sounds about right, huh."

Funny enough, that did kind of sum up their time in high school. Kids were obsessed with the opposite sex, wondering what it was like to make out or hook up, figuring it all out if they were in a relationship or in a position to do so. Such hormonal angst and pent up tension and frustration. That, of course, with the unfortunate day of the shooting and then the aftermath. It was always in the back of people's minds, in their deepest fears or their deepest fantasies. At least it was ever since the Washington Massacre.

"Want me to go first? Show you?"

She nodded.

Evan licked the salt off the rim, took the shot in one gulp, squeezed the juice out between his lips. He smirked, shifted over to her.

"Hmm."

Judith held up the shot glass, examined it like a scientist holding a small beaker. She was apprehensive but mustered the courage. She touched the tip of her tongue, tasting it, then licked a dollop off. She carefully swallowed the liquid, taking a while to finish, then sucked the wedge.

Evan watched as she did this, tracing her tongue and her lips, her almond eyes as she experienced it.

"Oh, and do the chaser too." He pointed at the glass of juice. "I didn't do mine, so you can have extra."

"You know, that wasn't too bad."

"Maybe a little faster next time. Actually 'shoot' it." Evan laughed. "You did the 'lick' and 'suck' part pretty great, though, if I do say so."

She hit him on the arm, light, lighthearted, leaning over.

As she sat upright, her hand touched his thigh by mistake. Her cheeks flushed pink.

"AHH!"

It was another loud groan of agony from Mark. The group responded in kind by laughing their asses off.

Between songs, Erin spoke through one cupped hand. "Now that we're all a little buzzed, or about to be. Everyone okay? Like, really okay?"

"Yeah, I think so. I'm good *now* . . ." Max tilted the beer, lifted it and chugged. "Fuck it."

"I'm glad no one got hurt, and that we're together." Judith shook her head, took a deep breath. "That's all that matters."

Huifang hugged her from the side.

Mark took one of the ice cubes from the pitcher to soothe his chest beneath his collar. He nodded, blinked.

"I mean . . ." Michelle turned to Erin then the group. "I gotta say, it's crazy that even happened. I'm still processing it."

"For reals."

Michelle rubbed the side of her neck. "Definitely not coming to the twenty-year."

A light round of laughter against the music, followed then by a hollow pause.

"Like, why us?" Evan chimed in without thinking.

The others waited for him to continue.

He thought about how much easier it would be to forget high school. Forget where it all started. Forget this awkward phase of life, the drama. Forget this horrific thing that happened to all of them—and is still happening.

Surviving this new attack reopened wounds from the old attack. For Max, it was a severed nerve. For Evan, it was faded scar tissue. For all of them, though, it was their psyche and repressed trauma.

"Just, it's not fair. And it's so not cool that we're this topic now. We, as a school, as a student body. This example. This talking point. You know? We're people. We were kids back then. I . . . I don't know . . . I just wanna be normal sometimes."

"Exactly."

"Amen to that."

They placed their glasses and bottles in the middle once again for another clink and cheers.

"Ooh!"

Huifang stood when the next song blasted.

"C'mon!"

Erin followed, waved to Michelle.

"Aw, no, I'm terrible at dancing—"

"So am I. Who cares. That's what the alcohol's for."

Judith turned to Evan. "Hey, you said it. We wanna be normal, right? Let's go and be normal. For one night. On one of the worst nights."

Evan smirked. Her eyes gazed right into his with the faintest sparkle, and her deep dimples poked through her cheeks.

"All right."

Motioning over to Mark and to Max, breathing in, he helped her up.

Huifang bent down to finish the rest of her mojito.

"Let's go dance this fuckin' night away."

❧

Awkward at first, they stood off to one side then began to loosen up. Max nodded along to the beat, closed his eyes and pumped a fist in the air. Mark bopped at his good shoulder, the movement wiggling its way down to his hips and his knees. Michelle and Erin held each other's hands, pushed and pulled in and out, in a rotating motion. Judith grooved in place with her arms out in front of her, with a wide smile, glancing at Evan who also started to nod, to bop, with a growing smirk. Huifang stepped in the middle, twerked and dropped low, shimmied as the bass kicked in.

They closer matched the energy of the bodies around them. The lasers and lights changed in pattern, as the background color faded then beamed out. Huifang pulled Mark into the middle, started to grind in front of him while Michelle and Erin started grinding in back, sandwiching him against his will.

"Get it!" Max shouted through the noise, started rocking along to the music, his flap cap about to come off. "Yeah!!!"

Evan and Judith faced one another, moving their bodies in rhythm, their eyes locked as the laser lights moved across their skin and their clothes. He scanned from her chest to her legs, peering through the darkened space as her hips mesmerized him. He slid closer as did she. Their hands came together and interlocked as they playfully moved in sync.

As they danced, their hands together, there was still a slight pause—shyness holding them both back, dividing lines and gray areas. An uncertainty. A moment of suspense that lingered. A tiny flicker of flame that whispered in their ear, drowning out the others on the dance floor and the rest of the club until it was just two of them floating, like how it used to once be upon a long lost time.

"Have a little fun!" Huifang shouted. "It's just dancing."

They both laughed at that, leaned closer, as if it were a permission slip.

Side to side, to the rhythm, she snapped her fingers while he clapped, both bending at the knees and swaying. Judith placed her hand on his shoulder, his arm. Evan reached around to the small of her back.

He remembered the two of them dancing at prom, but it

was so innocent back then. She in her dress and sandals. Him in his vest and tux.

He remembered the two of them dancing at the arcade, way back in the beginning. How she peeked over at him with a wide smile, laughing as she hopped on the tiles, doing a kind of spin move.

What's happening right now?

What are we . . .

The train of thought tapered as she now gazed up at him with a different look on her face. She tugged on the end of his tie, nibbling her bottom lip. Her chest and legs flashed in the darkness, their bodies blurred in movement, tempting him. He slid his palms, felt at her hips and torso and back through her clothes.

Judith grabbed his hand, turning around in place and wrapping it across her, pressed her back up against him. Her buttocks rubbed against his crotch. Evan gave in, pulled her tight. He breathed in her hair, felt the nape of her neck against his jaw and cheek. He slid his hands in front of her, where he could feel the raised lines from her undergarments.

For a good few songs in a row, they rocked on the dance floor. Max banged his head to one side, nodding along to the beat that was bumping. The three girls continued messing with Mark in various seductive moves and sensual poses. All the while, the two former lovebirds entwined and clung to one another like static.

The three girls went to the bar to order more drinks, which gave Mark the opportunity to take a breather and re-ice his shoulder. Max was joined by an attractive woman who sat on his lap and hugged him, to which he tilted back and spun around. It must have been the bartender friend of his. Evan took Judith by the hand, led her back to the cushioned seats.

"I'm just gonna rest my eyes." She plopped down, laying her head across his shoulder. "For a minute."

"Sure, go ahead."

He nuzzled his cheek against her, touched her shoulder, but caught himself. Maybe the alcohol was starting to wear off.

I don't deserve to be holding you right now.

I'm a piece of shit . . .

"Like we're back in school, huh." Mark grinned from across the table.

Evan laughed. "Hey, shut up. Who's the one with bitches all up on him?"

"All right, all right." He shook his head, put the ice cube and napkin down, slouched. "Don't mention a word to Kelly."

Evan pulled an imaginary zipper across his mouth, smirking.

"But seriously. Something goin' on with you two?"

"Nah, nah. Just catching up, having fun. And with everything that happened, maybe a temporary lapse. It's nothing."

Evan watched her as she breathed.

"I gotta say, though, phew . . ."

He arched his neck then shifted toward Mark.

"All this . . . It kinda does mess with my mind. She's just so . . . I kind of forgot, you know?"

"That puppy love."

"Puppy lust right now."

Both laughed, leaning forward with a sigh.

Mark shrugged. "You never know."

Evan blinked to himself, pondering that.

The three girls returned with more beer, another mojito and a second round of shots, started handing them out.

"Uh . . ." Evan raised a hand up, let out a nervous laugh. "I think she's done. I'm done."

Mark stared at the liquid in his hand, somber, sullen. A part of him was queasy. Another part was defeated.

"Okay, fine. I'll take his shot for him, but otherwise these two are done."

13

As the night came to an inevitable close, the group dispersed back to reality. The three girls who had way too much fun all hugged and said their goodbyes, walked back to their cars that were in different directions. Mark said he was gonna sober up in his car then head home, and not to worry about him. The pain in his shoulder had lessened by then, but he would go to the doctor in the morning to be certain. Max, the bartender friend, and a couple other new friends headed to the next place, some twenty-four hour diner. Evan offered to share a cab with Judith, make sure she got back safe, which she appreciated and obliged to in her happy sleepy state.

Evan held the door open, gestured to the driver who nodded.

"Be careful. Watch your step."

Judith hobbled out, taking his hand for balance.

He put his arm around her waist, still holding her hand as they walked up the steps to the lobby.

"Oh. Whoa, wow, those look sooo comfy . . ." Her voice was muttered, like a soft whisper from a half-lucid dream.

"Yes. They do." He also admired the soft white sofas and loveseats in the waiting area but continued on. "But you got a nice, wide bed waiting for you."

Her eyes closed for a second. "Mmm. That s-sounds greeat right about now."

"With big pillows, and a cool blanket. Right?"

From the elevator to the hall, they walked together, slow, steady, step by step. She fumbled for her key card. He held the door open for her as she slinked inside.

"Evan . . . Thank you . . ."

He leaned on the doorframe. "You're welcome."

Judith peeped up at him with her dazed almond eyes. "Not just for this, but for everything. For tonight."

"It was my pleasure." He smirked, tilted his head to kiss her on the cheek.

Not sure if it was their tipsy state, their tired state, but their faces lined up to where their lips almost touched, just off-center. He exhaled, leaned his forehead against hers.

Oh, man.

I'm so tempted.

Evan licked his lips, squeezed her hand again, then moved away. She seemed morose, faced down to her feet, clasping her hands.

He opened his mouth to speak, but just stared. Images of their dancing through the years flashed through his mind again: the arcade in freshman year, the prom in senior year, now the club at the reunion.

"Do . . ." Evan shook his head with a sigh. "D-do you wanna get . . . brunch?"

It was mixed nervousness, regret and shame asking that question that slipped from his subconscious out into the awkward moment.

Judith smiled back with a slow nod. That smile grew wide as she waved to him and closed the door. Evan himself couldn't help smiling as he turned and made his way down to the cab.

14

MANY THOUGHTS RAN through his mind as Evan awoke the next morning. He lay on the pillow, blinking, as the sun beamed through the window. The warmth felt good on his skin, and there was an odd peace in the quiet. He could hear birds chirping, hear a dog barking, along to the slow sound of cars passing through the near empty streets. His phone screen was packed full of notifications, missed calls and missed texts, voicemails. Jared had texted, worried, heard about what happened. Mark texted, and his doctor confirmed the contusion was severe but that it would heal with time, rest and ice. Michelle and Max both said they made it home all right. His parents and brother even tried to contact him. As he scrolled through each of these, about to respond, a new text popped up: Judith.

She wished him a good morning, with a happy face emoticon, then sent an accompanying selfie. It was her in her bed as well, on the pillow with the lit window behind her. Her lips appeared like candy in the screen in his hand. The sheen of her hair from that angle was angelic. It sent a flutter through his chest, and a cool shiver down his spine. The playful shot was as if he were in bed right next to her, and had woken up together. He sighed to himself and sent a selfie back, a funny face to which she replied, LOL, C U soon.

Ever since Evan sent that message online, they had almost automatically maintained this kind of fun, flirty, friendly rapport. He assumed it was natural amongst exes that kept in touch.

Adjusting the pillow, rolling over onto one side, he continued to linger, staring at her selfie staring back at him. Then he set a snooze alarm to take a short power nap.

Thoughts of dancing led to thoughts of dating. He remembered laying in the park. He remembered feeding the ducks by the stream, in their secret spot by the sideways tree. Remembered talking on the phone for hours. Remembered going to the carnival, and winning and carrying prizes and stuffed toys. He remembered making out, and pawing at and fondling one another on the floor of Max's mom's bedroom.

It was unclear whether it was a dream or a memory, but a certain scene began to unfold in his mind's eye . . .

The attendant tore the tickets, let both them in, pointing which way to go. Evan and Judith walked together hand in hand, a joyous bounce in their step. He asked her what she wanted and she kissed him on the cheek then again on the lips. All of his lunch money saved up burned in one concession order: soda, popcorn, candy.

They went up the short stairs to the side to their specified number theater, found an empty secluded area and sat down. She put her purse on the next seat, the big ol' bag of popcorn on top. He put the drink in his cup holder, the box of candy in hers. They giggled amongst themselves, joked, whispered, played with their fingers interlocked between them.

When the wide screen went dark, without hesitation they pounced on each other, lips parted, tongues writhing. He cupped her breast over her shirt, feeling the outline of her bra, as she rubbed over the zipper of his pants.

First, their heads tilted one way then the other, and they scooched closer. He slid his palm over her inner thigh as she touched his chest then his neck and the back of his head, caressing his hair. They paused to lick their lips, to catch their breath, then continued, their passion and movements intensifying.

Evan lost himself in that scene until, like the movie screen, it faded to black.

15

Hands on the steering wheel, he stared straight as the dream/memory replayed in bits and spurts. It was like a lava lamp or a kaleidoscope to him, beautiful and hypnotic. Evan leaned back on the headrest, slouched, breathing in, as a subtle somber and sullen feeling began to sink in. He swallowed a hard dry swallow, tightened his grip at ten and two. Was this a date? Was this a hangout? Was this even allowed? The passenger door clicked and flung open. As Judith hopped in, he adjusted and squirmed in place then straightened up.

Evan cleared his throat. "Good morning again."

"Hey." Judith smiled, buckling her seatbelt.

Although he tried not to, he found himself admiring her beauty. She was dressed more casual today, a fitted t-shirt with a swirly design and rhinestones that hugged around the curves in her chest, and cut-off jean shorts that showed her milky smooth thighs. Her hair was done up with a hair tie, stray strands hanging down.

"You're wearing glasses too?"

"I know, hehe. Just tired, from all the debauchery . . ." Her cheeks flushed, recalling and repressing everything that happened.

"My eyes are tired too." He watched as her tint of pink reddened, continuing to blush. "Look at us. You're like a librarian, and I'm like a professor."

She covered her face with her hands, laughed aloud. "I am so sorry if, like, it was weird last night, or over the line or anything—"

"No, it's totally fine. It was a long night, a strange night. We both were just relieved to be okay. It was pretty close there." Evan leaned in, raised an eyebrow. "Also, hey, not gonna complain. I got to dance with a very attractive woman."

"You enjoyed that, huh. Really."

"Eh, it was okay. Just so-so." Evan teased her, smirking.

"Liar. I could feel it."

They both laughed, faced away for a moment then returned. He gazed at her, their eyes meeting through the shiny reflections in their frames, his thick-rimmed and rectangular, hers thin and round.

"Seriously, though. I assure you. All in good fun. Rated PG-13. Nothing too inappropriate or over the line."

Judith inclined her head, their eyes locking. "Such a gentleman."

This banter continued as they pulled away from the hotel, through the city streets, into the upscale area with boutiques and shops and restaurants, a bright green and breezy park with a big playground out front.

Again, a city is so much a garden of concrete. It has this energy and life all its own, and continually grows and changes. For a long many years, the area had been an empty lot then a construction site, closed off, covered up, but now was booming. Other areas that were once decent or nice, meanwhile, became overrun by graffiti and tent cities and abandoned cars, with businesses shutting down and buildings remaining vacant.

"So much has changed, huh?"

"Yeah. Seriously." Evan also glanced out the window as they pulled up to the red light, waiting to turn.

"It's kinda nice being home. I'd move back."

"Hmm. Would you?"

When they parked and walked to the escalators, he noticed his graphic tee and khakis complemented her outfit. As they passed by couples and families, they appeared to fit right in, blending with the atmosphere.

It was just past that peak time for brunch so they lucked out and were seated right away. Artsy decor adorned the tables, intricate pieces hung on the walls. Lighting fixtures suspended from black wires, modern and elegant, setting the perfect dimness and perfect ambiance.

Judith scanned the interior, then peeked at the menu. "This is so crazy. One minute, life is this mundane thing, and then another . . . It's like I traveled through a time warp, almost unbelievable."

"I know. This isn't how I expected my Saturday to go." Just his eyes showed from behind the menu. "But, hey, I'll take it."

This interaction, this encounter, was something of a happy bittersweet accident. If either had come with someone else, would they have been able to catch up the way that they did? If there wasn't adrenaline pumping in their veins, would they have danced together and drank together?

"Came a long way since we used to have Chemistry."

"We still have chemistry." Her eyes sparkled as she said this, the tip of the straw passing between her lips.

An exchange of laughter between them.

"Of course . . ." Evan tapped the tabletop with his fingers. "Do you remember one of the first things from when we studied back then?"

"What?"

"I always hated that class. But there was one thing that kinda stuck with me, even 'til now." He raised a finger up before continuing. "When things 'change,' nothing is ever lost."

Judith leaned her cheek in her palm, letting it sink in.

Her eyes shifted from staring right at him to staring right above him. He turned around, wondering what it was. One of the other patrons held a newspaper in hand, followed the hostess, with the headline big and bold.

DISASTER AT WASHINGTON REUNION:
ATTEMPTED SHOOTING UNSUCCESSFUL,
4 INJURED

Evan stood and walked from the tables to the long counter. He reached over the empty stool to a stack of newspapers that were complimentary.

He came back, turned it sideways between them, like they used to do with the textbook before in class. She placed her pretty fingernail below the first word in the first sentence, and he followed it as they read along.

Graduates from President George Washington High School participated in their ten-year reunion last night. The Eagles, Class of 2002, had been survivors of a deadly coordinated shooting in their senior year which already prompted high alert from government officials, law enforcement and event planners. Armed security was present at the venue, covering all areas and points of access. However, despite extensive preparation and preventative measures, the alumni would be endangered still. While attendees began to enjoy the presentation, festivities and meal from the buffet, an armed gunman crashed a gray pickup truck through the barricade, breaching the outside perimeter and landing in a concrete ditch. Witnesses described the motion of the vehicle as intentional, appearing to swerve left and right in an attempt to injure security present. The shooter then entered the Crescent Ballroom from the southwest entrance, wearing a backpack and body armor, carrying an AR-15 style rifle and multiple magazines. Using smoke grenades, the shooter attempted to break into the event hall but was met with security who opened fire. In the exchange, four guards sustained mild injuries and are now at Regal North Hospital in stable condition.

The alleged gunman was taken into custody and has been identified as nineteen-year-old Antonio Felipé Casilla. Initial reports state that Casilla was transfixed by the original Washington Massacre event and idolized Derek Harrison, Cheng-Fai Ho and Adrian Lorenza. Other than this link found through journal entries and online search history, a specific motive remains undetermined at this time. Casilla is said to have a long history of anger management and behavioral issues, as well as possible undiagnosed ADHD and schizophrenia. Past social media posts can be seen with the suspect holding a variety of weapons, and making hateful and threatening statements including claiming to harm and kill animals. In the latest update from an evening press conference with the governor, civic leaders, and top police and school district officials, it was revealed that Casilla shot both of his adoptive parents prior to the attack. As the investigation is currently ongoing, more details of this tragic event will be released. In a closing statement, the governor commended the response team and conveyed his gratitude that members of the graduating class were fortunately unharmed.

☙

Although it indicated the story continued on page A6, they both had read enough. Evan leaned back, crossed his arms and placed his elbows on the table. Judith straightened up, clasped her palms and touched her chin to them. Between the big, bold headline and the start of the article was a photo of the suspect. The shooter had pale skin and big ears, their eyes mixed with glare and shock. Thick and wide glasses hung from the crook of his nose, amplifying the eyes even more. He had medium length curly hair that swept off his stern brow. His dark orange jumpsuit appeared more like something from a mental asylum than the county lockup.

"So, this is the bastard that almost killed Mark . . ."

"They didn't include that in the article, huh." She shook her head. "I mean, all the details will come out soon, I'm sure. Another media circus. Just like last time."

Evan took a slow sip of water. "Yeah. But at least we're all breathing, mild injuries or not. I'm glad it was stopped before getting too bad, and they actually got the guy. Like, if what happened back then happened again, to that same extent, I don't know if anyone could take it."

"You're right. Oh, I spoke to the police this morning. Did you get a call?"

"They left a message. I'll call later or something. Not quite ready to talk. It was enough texting everybody back, calling my brother then my parentals."

Judith sighed. "It was pretty hard talking to my mom and dad about it."

"Definitely. That's the part an article, a report, whatever program, would never be able to convey. The real impact of something like this."

"I feel like . . ." Her voice began to crackle. "People just don't care enough, sadly. Time and time again, these atrocities happen. Some are bigger, some are smaller. But there's this story, chatter for a little while, and then nothing changes."

"Yeah, it's hard. Kind of a taboo topic to most." He faced down then faced back up. "Which is so freaking dumb. How do you ever expect to solve a problem if you can't even talk about it?"

"Exactly."

This train of thought weaved in and out of the conversation, between catching up and small talk and eating. He had eggs benedict, she had huevos rancheros. He had a screwdriver. She had a mimosa.

On the next table over, an older married couple also both wore glasses and read the newspaper between them.

Look at that.

Judith ate a little too much, she said, and suggested they take a walk after. They went past some commercial office buildings, a coffee shop and a bubble tea spot, to an area by the stream with benches lined. She picked one out with enough shade, and he sat down next to her.

It was a beautiful scene with ducks in formation creating little ripples on the surface of the water. Down the walking path, there were two dogs playing and their two owners laughing. A flock of greenish birds flew from one tree to the next.

"You think about it a lot?"

"Probably too much, honestly." Evan thinned his lips, furled his brow. "Wanna say every day, but nah, almost every day."

She shifted towards him, tilted her head. "You been through more than most. And you never did tell anyone, what really happened. Other than me . . ."

"Eh, what does it matter."

"You never did take credit, either. How it was you that undid those chains, helped everybody out of the gym and out of the cafe . . ."

Judith placed her hand over his, squeezing his hand and his knee at the same time. Evan moved his fingers, touching her fingertips, glancing at her. The reflection in her almond eyes matched the sparkles on the water.

All these years later, a full decade, and here they both were, holding hands and sitting together on a bench.

She sighed and laid her head on his shoulder.

Just two old friends catching up. That's all.

This is nothing.

"I . . . I hope this is okay."

He nodded, swallowed.

"This feels so nice. To forget everything. Forget all the pressures. Forget all of the questions."

Evan smirked. "It does."

A slight gust swept through, blowing along with it a few leaves and a single flower with hues of white and red.

He bent down, picked it up and handed it. "Funny, huh? We're on the other side of the stream now. Literally."

"I noticed, hehe. We used to hang right over there, at that park. Sit on the swings." She twirled the flower in her hand as if it were a mini-pinwheel. "And school was down that way, where the stream forks."

Both moved closer in, got more cozy and comfortable, as the clouds glided overhead.

With the sky and the air and the birds, the water, the quiet, it was the perfect moment. A much needed tranquil, serene, calm escape. Had things been different, he would have leaned in and kissed her right then and there. He did mull it over in his mind but decided against it. No, this would have to do, walking that dangerous thin line of flirtation between old lovers.

"If I never told you, I can tell you now . . . And if I already did, I'll tell you again . . . I think you're amazing, Evan." Judith breathed in and out, adjusted her head on his shoulder. "What you did. What you've carried, this whole time. You're, like, a hero."

"Thank you." He leaned his jaw against the top of her head. "You know, I don't really feel like that, though. I feel like . . ."

"Like what?"

"Everything that happened was my fault."

Her eyes screwed upward to gaze at him. "We've talked about this. It had been years at the time, that's just not true. At all. You didn't pull the trigger. You didn't load the clips in. You had nothing to do with those other two, either."

"I-I know that. But still, it torments me." Evan grinded his teeth. "I can't help this sinking feeling, like a cloak. Like a cloud over me. I don't deserve happiness."

She wrapped one arm behind his back. "And this is why you broke up with me?"

"It was a lot of things." His feet bounced off the ground. His fingers started to clench, to tremble.

Judith was quiet, waited to hear more.

"I cared about you so much I didn't wanna hold you back. You had to live your dream, had to go and do amazing things. I wanted you to be the absolute happiest that you could be."

"Are you?"

Evan tilted his chin down with a *hrmm* sound.

"Happy?"

"Been a while since anybody asked me that. Ah, what's happiness. Right?"

She wrapped her other arm across his torso, held him. "That can't be. Everybody wants to be happy. And you do deserve it, you do."

He gave in, laid his arm across her shoulder blades.

"You remember graduation? It actually drizzled that day. I remember such melancholy, being so far from all right. Then the sun came out, and there was this big rainbow. It happened during my speech. Everything vanished, melted away. There was all this hope. There was peace. A calm after the storm."

He closed his eyes, sighed, rubbed her upper arm.

"I want that for you. Your rainbow, Evan."

There was a long pause where they just embraced, just existed.

Maybe they should have said this years ago. Maybe they could still be together, if he wasn't wracked with guilt, if he didn't choose to take it on by himself. Maybe she could have tried a little harder to get him to open up, to not let him go. It's not easy, life and love, growing up, growing apart, not to mention with what happened.

"And you? Are you happy, Jude?"

She stared, blinked. "I'm not unhappy. But at the same time, I did always feel like I wanted to be deliriously happy. Things are okay, sure, and yet, I wonder if something is missing. Something might be off."

"The rest of your life's a pretty long time."

"Haha. You used to always say that."

"I know what you mean, though. Small confession . . . I know not every relationship is gonna be your high school sweetheart, but I do compare sometimes. What we had was so real, you know? Like, worth throwing everything away for. I'd do it all over in a heartbeat."

"We should've fought harder, I think. To save us." A tear gathered in the corner of her eye. "To save each other."

Evan felt his own eyes water but fought it back. He nodded, smirked.

Most of the time on that bench was spent in silence. Their smartphones didn't ring. They didn't message anyone or check social media, had nowhere to go and no one to see. It was like before, when times were simpler and made a lot more sense. Them being together still made sense, he thought but kept to himself. Repressed it like so many other thoughts and feelings.

He suggested that she take a nap, get some rest before dinner with her parents. They drove the scenic route back, reminiscing along the way.

Judith placed her hand on the handle, clicked it open but stopped in place. He glanced over as she turned around, their eyes locking.

"D-do you . . . wanna meet up again? Tomorrow?"

Huh.

One night is turning into a whole weekend.

"I . . . I would love that." He tapped the steering wheel as if it were a drum. "There is this one thing. I wasn't sure I even wanted to go, but tomorrow's the last day. If you're interested."

She smiled a wide smile, her deep dimples showing.

16

As they walked along the pathway then up the steps, they didn't say much. Perhaps it was because there was too much to say, to think. Perhaps they had already said most of it. The grass had been freshly cut and the chlorophyll scent filled his nostrils, reminding him of school. Evan glanced over at Judith, admired her hair and her makeup. She wore a light blouse, a bit frilly, and tight white pants that hugged her legs and buttocks. He had a black vest on and khakis, the cuffs of his long sleeve collar shirt rolled up. Both dressed more fancy than usual for the special occasion. On either side of the entrance were large stone statues that Judith glanced at, inclining her head. He paid for their tickets, then let her pass through the turnstile first.

"Hey. Thanks for picking me up again."

Evan walked with his hands in his pockets. "No biggie."

"And thanks for saying yes too. Glad we're together a second time."

"Yeah, it's been forever. It could be another long while, if at all. We're having such a good time, why not."

There was a courtyard with more statues, these copper and bronze, and some glass display cases. Couples and groups walked along slow, admiring the pieces.

Judith smiled. "Never did anything like this back then."

"Right. Guess it was different, huh? More going to the movies, renting movies. Hanging at the mall. I kind of do miss that. Miss playing video games and listening to music, reading comic books and stuff, manga."

"Our nerd lives."

He chuckled. "I mean, we're all still geeks at heart. Just got a lot more going on, more outgoing. Less time to indulge in such things."

"Well, this is nice. Great suggestion." She walked up to the display case, hunched over it. "Never get to go on dates like this."

The artifacts were displaced from their time period, forgotten and lost, should have deteriorated over the years and decades. But here they were, cleaned up, restored to their original condition, perfect.

They made their way to the left wing, the first exhibit. As they entered, it was like a maze with different rooms and corridors lined with painting after painting.

One of the first that drew them in was a ship with red sails amongst splashing waves and puffs of cloud. Another was of birds flying in formation in the sky. Evan perused with his hands behind his back.

"What do you look at, when you look at these?" Judith gestured with her hand. "Like, what is it you see?"

"I mean, art is art. The whole point. Whatever emotion or reaction you get, that's the real deal. There's no wrong way to appreciate something."

She smiled, stepped over to the next.

"There is a lot to consider, though. From the frame to the mat, sometimes double or triple mat. All deliberate choices. The colors and the shadows. The depth." Evan waved his fingers over each area as he pointed these out. "I like to see the brush strokes. You can tell when it was carefully, thoughtfully done. Or if it was done in a flurry, in almost anger."

"You never did tell me, you know . . ."

He paused, turned towards her.

"What ever happened with that art contest?"

Evan's smirk stretched into a half-smile. "First place."

Ceramic pieces were on display on a big round table. There were flowers, vases, a cat, a doll, a tiny dancer. Another table had wooden slabs with ink blots on it or carved in. There were masks on the wall behind that, some tribal and some festive like from a stage play.

Different areas had different themes. Paintings on one side were abstract, the faces and bodies mismatched and choppy, as if from out of a dream. Others were of a serious subject with a serious expression in a straightforward portrait. There was also a self-portrait, a woman with a prominent brow and blanketed in gold. Some of the pieces were large, could cover an entire ceiling. Some were a tidal wave, or a wave of color amongst the night sky.

"You should play us something." Evan gestured with his chin to a grand piano in the corner, a velvet rope and sign in front.

Judith covered her mouth with her hand. "Oh, no, I don't think we're that mischievous anymore."

Both laughed a hushed laugh, continued to peruse the exhibit.

"I do miss that. One of my fave things."

She gazed down, hiding back a smile.

The right wing was more pop art, inspired by retro posters and tin cans. Some were all splotches and splatters, drizzles and drips. A whole back wall was selections of stylized graffiti.

Some were upside down. Some were in bits and pieces like a collage, with foil.

There were various statues, some historical, some cultural or religious. Several were nude and erotic. One piece hanging was of burnt wood and molten glass. Then, of course, more paintings.

". . . I'm not sure if this house is far away, or if it's a tiny house."

Much to the dismay of those around them, they let out the loud laugh they had been trying to hold in. That was a good point to take a break, they decided. Evan led them to a sitting area with light refreshments and snacks before entering the next exhibit in the back building of the museum.

"You ready to fly tomorrow?"

"Don't know. I can't quite think that far right now. Just trying to be in the moment, I guess." Judith held her paper cup with two hands, dazed. "We got the hotel room to not impose on my parentals, except the last night, but it's kinda weird by myself."

Evan took a deep breath.

"Forces you to do some much needed reflection. When it's so quiet like that."

"Nervous?"

"More like apprehensive? Not sure of what I want, or something. Like you said, the rest of your life's a pretty long time."

He swallowed, placed his hand on the table. "I could be mistaken. But maybe it shouldn't be so difficult. It should be easy. It should make sense. Try not to think about it."

Judith gazed back, nibbling her lower lip.

"You know . . . Do you wanna get outta here? Maybe I can show you something, actually. I just decided."

<h1 style="text-align:center">17</h1>

UNLIKE THE MUSEUM that was clean and organized, was separated into neat sections that made sense, his apartment was sprawling and chaotic. Evan felt some regret taking Judith there as he held the door open and let her in. Paint cans were scattered all over the floor, covered in plastic tarps in some places. There was a ladder turned sideways over a large canvas. Paint brushes and palettes and tubes of paint lay on newspapers on the counter by the kitchen. She panned her head from left to right with her jaw hanging open and her eyes wide, taking a slow step forward. He walked in front, yanked off white sheets that covered some of the easels. Evan watched her take another step, panning back from right to left.

"S-sorry it's such a mess. I—"

"This is incredible."

Evan almost scoffed, the sound trapped in his esophagus. He mustered a smirk in return.

She passed from one piece to the next, floating on her feet.

"When did you . . . ?"

"If you remember, I used to always draw and sketch." He followed, stood next to her as she glanced down at one of the works in progress. "I stopped doing anything like that, after what happened. Never touched a pencil to paper. Forgot all about it."

"Amazing." She raised her fingers to her face in astonishment.

"Sometime after we broke up, which could have been a mistake . . ." Evan sighed, hung his shoulders low. "Well, I started drawing again, which led me to all this. I'm not sure why. Not sure where I am going with it, even now."

She stepped over scattered supplies to another painting, stared up at it, felt the dried layers of paint and the brush strokes with her fingertips.

"I started with watercolor. I tried acrylic. But as you can see, I kind of settled on oil. I mean, I'll do whatever I want. I'm free here." He licked his lips, tiptoed around the tarp. "Free from the future or from the past, the present. Free from regret. Free from worry, concern. Truly free."

Judith shook her head. "You used to be more of an open book, you know. Wore your emotions right on your sleeve."

Evan joined her in the rays of sunlight that passed from the window. Judith appeared like a ballet figure twirling on a music box, captivating.

"All of this, it almost seems like your inner life to me. What you've been holding back, pushing away deep down. Your true self."

He tilted his head, crossed his arms.

"I guess I, uh . . . needed something." He felt slight water rush over his eyes, blinked. "There's just something about trying to put together an image, a color. Taking it from the deepest, darkest parts of your soul, bit by bit, out into the real world."

"Could this be it?"

"Hmm?"

"Your rainbow."

They stared into one another's eyes, the sunlight engulfing them both like magic.

"I-I-I don't know, what I'm doing or what this all means." He swallowed. "Wish I did. Honestly."

Her tongue peeked from behind her teeth as she considered her next words. "Yeah. I see it. I can feel it."

For a brief moment, their teenage versions flashed in the illuminated space.

"This is as good or better than anything we saw today."

"Really?"

"You're an artist, Evan. You always have been, though you may not have known it, or even forgot. You should pursue this."

"What? Become a painter? Seems so impossible." He faced down to the floor. "I wouldn't even know where to start."

"It starts right now."

Versions of them in their teens returned to versions of them in their twenties, close enough to interlock at the fingers.

"This is your first gallery showing." She pointed past him, playful, upbeat. "What's that one there?"

He exhaled through pursed lips, slid a box over to make some room. "This is the face of a homeless man that frequents this area. I see him around the bus stop a lot, pushing his cart around. Poor guy."

"Oh, wow. This is exquisite work."

"I give him some change sometimes, got him a soda. But there's something about his face. You can almost, like, see God in there."

"And, Mister Big Ah-teest, which one's your crown jewel?"

He smirked, touched his hand to the small of her back as he guided her through the space. Her eyes turned up like little crescent moons in excitement.

They moved from the well lit warmth to a dim cool corner. A lone easel at an angle was emphasized as they moved closer toward it. The splashes of color popped off the canvas. The shade, the depth, the tone and imagery all drew her in like a vortex.

It was a heart shape doused in a fiery burst, melting away in an upward diagonal motion against a dark royal blue with white speckles. Pink, purple, yellow, orange streaks and waves weaved in and out, blended and blurred.

"Been at this one for a few months. Just finished."

"This is a masterpiece. Extraordinary."

Evan stood still, rubbed his chin and scratched his head.

"What was it that you were thinking? What were you feeling then, when you made this?"

"A so-called love, I suppose."

Judith turned to him, perked up, listened.

"When you're falling in love, your heart is floating, up high, weightless, in the vastness of space. And if that love is lost, you come flying back down through the ozone. You may collide, ignite and crackle, land on rough terrain, bounce around and around until there is another heart doing the exact same thing at the exact same time. And then, well, you float once again."

He could feel her soften to that, lower her head then face forward with a deep breath in and out. She shifted, opened her mouth to speak.

"I have to tell you something . . ." Judith twisted on the ball of her foot, fidgeted with her fingers. "Ever since you sent me that first message, all these feelings came racing back. And now, spending all this time, I . . ."

What?

What are you saying?

"Like, I might still be hung up on you, after all this time."
She closed her eyes as she took a verbal leap of faith. "It was
you who first spoke your feelings back then, so maybe it's my
turn now."

"Jude, no—"

"Let me say this. Please. I know i-it's crazy. It is. Yes. But I
can't help it. I mean, maybe not right this very second, but we
could think about it, talk about it." Judith inclined her head,
sighed. "I just always felt like there was something missing,
and I haven't felt that way these past few days, nights. These
past how many months, looking forward to our little back-
and-forth online."

Evan shook his head, kicked at the floor.

"Like you said, what we used to have, what we could still
have . . . It's worth throwing everything to the wind for. And I
think I'd be willing to take that chance. I have to know for sure
the one I end up with is the right one. Zero doubts."

So much new information overloaded his circuits. He
remained frozen with his arms at his sides, stared ahead with
a blank expression.

Is this real?

Could we really try again? Get it right this time?

Do I deserve this?

Do I deserve . . . her?

No.

No, I don't. I can't. I'm a piece of shit!

"I ain't no medical director, Jude. I didn't go to grad
school. Don't got a fancy car, don't got a big house. I'm a
freaking penniless artist at best, and I have not a damn thing to
offer you. I think I knew that even before." He turned around,
held his forearm across his eyes, trying to fight back everything
overflowing as if a concrete dam had crumbled. "I'm broken.

I'm lost. Jude, I'm nothing. I am less than nothing, and will always be."

"No. If anyone can be successful, it's you. It's the truth. You have this special something inside you that makes you different." She put her hand on his shoulder, patted then rubbed it. "Whatever pain or personal anguish, it makes you stronger, better for it. You can turn it around and use it. And, also, you don't have to go through this by yourself."

As she slid her palm down to this chest, she could feel his heart beating. Judith blinked, watched him.

"You were always so quick to want to save me, to wanna protect me. No matter what. Even the other night still . . . Let me do that for you, Evan."

He closed his eyes, tensed up. His fingers trembled and his teeth grinded.

18

Tossing, turning, unable to sleep, Evan didn't know where to go or what to do, but wanted to try to clear his mind. A gust of breeze blew steady against him, was ice cool in the pitch black, as he climbed over the gate then walked up the small incline winding around the cemetery grounds. Evan kept his hands in his pockets, faced down to his feet as he passed the obvious NO TRESPASSING sign. He could hear his own footsteps, hear his own breath. It was somehow peaceful although it was a bit creepy. His foot tripped on the edge of the path but he caught himself, struggled to make his way amongst the near invisible shades and lines and shapes, refraining from using the light from his phone. Evan bumbled forward, blind. The night is darkest just before the dawn, as the saying goes.

Plopping down, he placed both elbows on both knees, leaned forward.

"I should, uh, pour a forty out or something, huh . . ."

Evan let out a nervous laugh. He realized all of a sudden how absurd it was that he spoke out loud to the air, to himself, and to his long lost best friend.

"All right. Anyway. I'm . . . I'm sorry it's taken me so long to come and visit. I went to the funeral, but that was hard enough. Not sure what I'm doing out here. This is probably the first and last time, if I'm being honest, Der. It's just been such a weird few days. Few months, few years. Few lifetimes."

He glanced up at the night sky that was clear.

"Most people call you a monster, will never forgive you. Some people call you a tragic trainwreck, a misunderstood and unfortunate soul. I myself, in a way, land maybe somewhere in between, maybe all of the above."

His body slumped, slouched in position with his head and shoulders down.

"I kind of fucking hate you, for all that you did. What you did to me. What you did to school, to everybody. To Jude . . . To Max . . ."

Max always said he had trouble recalling the details as it all happened so fast. But perhaps Max did know but chose to keep it secret, the same way Judith was the one person who knew who stabbed Evan. Some things were better left unsaid, unexplained.

"On that same note, though, I do miss you. I carry this weight around, this deep sense of remorse, of regret. But I don't think I can anymore. I don't think I should. And I just don't want to." He shook his head, faced away. "I'm done. Done suffering. Done blaming myself. I want to live my life. I wanna be free . . . I want to be . . ."

As he adjusted, he felt hard metal press against the side of his thigh.

"Hey, look. I still got it. I've kept it, this whole entire time. I figured I'd bring it here, just felt right."

Evan played with the butterfly knife—swish, swish, flick, click—held it in his hand, stared at it, squeezed it, feeling the circular holes in the handle, then put it away after an extended moment of silence.

"I guess that's it, dude." He sighed, stood to his feet. "I'm mad, most of all mad. I'm sad too. I am pretty damn messed up." With a shrug, he nodded to himself. "But I think it may finally be time to try to let go, to move on. It's been long enough. Ten years is way long already."

When he returned to the car and slammed the door shut, all at once, the hot tears came rolling down the side of his cheeks. His lips curled and trembled as he began to whimper and sob, his breathing stifled, out of his control. Evan banged the steering wheel with a closed fist, hard, yelled at it, banged it again and again. He leaned his head into the cushion then stared at his own reflection staring back, relaxed his muscles. There was still sniffling in between hyperventilating, but it subsided as he regained his composure. Turning the key, then turning the wheel, he started to drive without thinking, without feeling.

The white and yellow lines, dotted, solid, double solid, rolled on like an endless loop. It reflected back as the headlights shined over the short distance ahead in the darkness. Unsure where the road was taking him, he somehow hit green light after green light. Evan pulled up the steep hill, winded through the back streets, passed along the neighborhoods at the base of the mountain, then headed down to the city again.

He jerked the wheel with a hard sudden screech, slammed on the brake. Up in the sky, for a split second, there was a white flash and a tiny blip of color. He opened the door, gazed up from the road.

Was that a . . . comet?

A shooting star?

In the corner of his naked eye, he saw a rapid splice through the air like a focused beam of light. Burning through the upper layers of the atmosphere, with ionized elements shining in radiant streaks of red and violet, of green and blue-green amidst a glowy neon white like a diamond. He had never seen anything like that before. His heart thudded in his chest. The hairs raised on his arms and on the back of his neck.

Evan staggered back, scanned his surroundings. With the car door open, headlights beaming, he was right behind the fields of Washington. Next to him was the arch of the bridge above the stream, where they used to pass by countless times after school. Him and Derek. Mark, Jared, Max. Judith. In that same spot, part of the candlelight vigil was held a decade earlier.

The earlier conversation played in his mind.

"I-I-I just don't know. Is this such a good idea?"

"It's okay, Evan. I'm scared too. But I know it can work this time. I'll wait. I'll wait for you, a little while. There's time left, but not too much." She took his hand, squeezed it. "We'll talk when you're ready. Or, you know, maybe be like the old Evan and do some great, big, hopeless romantic grand gesture."

Jude . . .

He wrapped his arms around her, held onto her tight like he used to. Like he meant it. Like it mattered. Like it was the end of world and their impending doom.

Her perfume, her lips hovering right next to his collar bone, her bosoms pressed up against his chest, it was exhilarating. That electrical charge shot through every nerve in his body.

Snapped back to current reality, Evan noticed his hands in mid-air as if she were right there. Except there was nothing, and it was cold and empty.

Could this actually happen?

His feet dragged across the asphalt backwards until the

small of his back tapped into the fender. Visions of a possible future flashed through his mind like clairvoyance. They joined hands over the table, fed each other dessert. They announced the news to the others, were greeted with cheers and hugs. The two rearranged furniture, balanced out the feng shui in their new home. The two were on an airplane, were in a fancy pool area. He waited at the end of the aisle, watched her walk down toward him. They got the news from the doctor, held the ultrasound print in their hands with teary smiles.

19

Taking out one large backpack and then a small tote bag, the screen door rattled behind her as it closed shut. Judith tucked away her flight itinerary then carried the luggage down the small steps in front of the house, with careful controlled movements. He gazed at her from the sidewalk, a crooked smile creeping across his face. She got to the trunk then flinched, did a double take. Evan stepped forward, lifted up the colorful bouquet. The old Evan as she referred would have picked them from someone else's garden and gotten yelled at, would have run across town through sprinklers and busy streets to get to her, even for a mere five minutes. This new Evan settled for store bought behind-the-counter stuff and then taking a short spontaneous drive.

"Oh my God. Evan, this . . ."

"Hey, Jude."

As she walked over the lawn, she noticed the pavement in front of him covered in colored chalk.

His smile widened as he gestured for her to join him. She took the flowers in one hand, wrapped her arm in the crook of his elbow as he led them along. Beneath their feet, the drawings sprawled on and overlapped, interconnected in a long mural all around the block. It was big poofy clouds and then flocks of birds, lush mountains, schools of fish. Flowers, fruits. Hearts, balloons, streamers, confetti. Anthropomorphic rabbits and cats. Mustachioed characters from one of his favorite video games and ninjas wearing headbands from one of his favorite anime. Flames, skulls, missiles and explosions. Superheroes, supervillains. A banyan tree. Waves on the beach. All of the planets lined and a satellite, a spaceship. An imploding star. A dinosaur. There were spiders as well as spiderwebs. There was spaghetti. There was a soda can. There was a machine gun. Then it was the cityscape along the horizon, with rain and with lightning, the tops of buildings and skyscrapers looming over the streets with cars passing and pedestrians carrying umbrellas. Then it was a carnival tent. Then it was lily pads on the surface of the water. Then it was a ring and the words, I LOVE YOU.

Judith walked in awe as they followed this long stream of consciousness to the very end, where a happy tear formed in the corner of her almond eye. Primary and secondary colors pierced the everyday mundane ground that they walked on and took for granted, transforming it into something fantastic, whimsical and spectacular, from out of this world.

"I thought a lot about what you said, and no. No, it's you. It has always been you."

"Huh?"

Evan turned, faced her, held her at the hips.

"My rainbow."

Both leaned in, touched the crest of their foreheads together, pulled each other close and held onto one another. They could feel the crispness of the morning air. They heard the birds sing in the branches of the trees. She glanced up in his eyes, pouted her lips and pressed them to his, a light and unsure touch like they were inexperienced teenagers again.

AFTERWORD

For a long time, I debated whether or not to ever try to publish this collection. A few of these pieces were from my early days as an aspiring writer, still learning the craft and learning my own process. Over time, there were so many signs to go through with it that I could no longer ignore it. There was a double rainbow that stretched before my eyes on my apartment balcony while holding my toddler. There was the last picture taken on my friend's cell phone before he passed away (to whom this book is dedicated) of a full rainbow arc over the church across the street from our neighborhood. A hundred other little things occurred along the way that I can't even list them all. Not to mention, quite a few fans wanted more from my debut novel, and two of these stories are related.

The first story I wrote, "Hemingway Dorks and the Jurassic Rock," is one that goes back to my ENG100 class in college. I had written it as an assignment and the professor liked it and pushed me to submit to the school literary journal, which it was accepted and printed. I got a lot of compliments on that original work. I completely rewrote it from scratch, using everything I had been studying and practicing, changed some of the character and place names, tweaked the title. It is a short piece so it sat in a binder on the shelf for a long time, until now.

The second story I wrote, "Reach for New Heights," is one

that I actually wrote for a short story competition in Writer's Digest. I was trying to push myself and get my name out there, unsuccessfully of course. One big thing was that the requirements for the competition only allowed for 1500 words. I had shown my brother the original version. He enjoyed it but said it was a little short, which I agreed. Years later, I rewrote it without limitations of any kind, and am much happier with the end result, as is my brother. To me, climbing a mountain like in the story has become a kind of metaphor for writing. I felt so inadequate, so unprepared, out of my league, an imposter. But over time, with enough effort, here I am today.

My novelette, *Tate the Elephant,* was kind of a happy accident. My friend and fellow writer Tate, also the namesake of this story, told me about a film pitch competition. It was something like $250,000 for a synopsis of 250 words. Of course, I thought why not, mostly as an exercise. This idea came to me after watching a documentary of an incident that occurred in my hometown when I was a young child—I barely remember it myself, but the images were ingrained in my brain of an elephant barreling through the streets. I wrote the 250 words, but there was no life in them. It read like a Wikipedia entry. So I ditched the competition and instead expanded it into what became my first novelette and my first seemingly decent writing. I felt proud of this one compared to anything else I had written at the time. There was a sort of magic that sparked on the page and almost wrote itself. I eventually showed this to my writing partner, beta readers, my brother, my wife, and there was a lot of good feedback. They were curious to see where this story would end up, were impressed by the characters and the dialogue, and were all saddened by the end. For the first time, I too felt sad. I never felt that before and still feel that today. These characters were alive.

The fourth story I wrote, "Inbound," is one that had been in my head for a while. It was national news in 2018 when that infamous text message alert was sent out and led to many confused and terrified people. Now, luckily, this was just a mistake and an embarrassment and an unfortunate half an hour or so. But what if it was real? Or what if it had been worse? I myself like the protagonist missed the text message, didn't even get it. I saw it on social media after, when things had already calmed down. This was my way of exploring this and experiencing this, but in a much more dramatic fashion. Over time, composite sketches of the concept and the characters all came to me: a boy, a dog, an old man, a pregnant woman. I wanted it to be an unlikely hero and this mismatched group.

My novella, *Washington Reunion,* has been a long time coming. I don't know why, but I always had the idea to see where these characters would be in ten years. I wanted to write about grief and trauma, about the long-term effects of such a tragedy. I thought about how close friends drift away or how their relationship changes. I thought about the idea of exes, too, and lingering feelings of the so-called one. There were also some intentionally unanswered questions in my debut novel that I got to answer here, though many still I will take to the grave. I didn't have too much ironed out before I sat down at the keyboard for this one. All I knew was that the two love interests would be broken up, that the main character still had old feelings and there were complications there. I knew the one survivor would have PTSD, suicidal thoughts and substance abuse issues. I didn't know that there would be an action sequence. I didn't know the two love interests would have a chance to reconnect. That all just happened on the page.

The title of this collection and a subtle connected theme is of rainbows. In my hometown, there is pretty much a rainbow every day. I played with that notion, since a couple stories are loosely tied to local events that happened. Rainbows are beautiful, in terms of aesthetics but also in their meaning and depth, even in the science. I remember sneaking into my friend's class in high school. This was in the final weeks before graduation so it was kind anything goes and whatever by then. But the lesson on rainbows and refraction that day stood out to me, stuck with me all this time. Even as a kid, I used to borrow books from the library about light and reflection and about prisms, and just be in awe. Rainbows go back to the bible and the story of the ark and the covenant. Rainbows go back to Aristotle. It can be argued there is still much mystery surrounding the phenomenon of rainbows. There are double, triple rainbows. There are circular rainbows. There are rainbows at night, in fog and in ice and in snow, possibly on the moon of Saturn. You can see rainbows in the slick of an oil puddle. There are rainbow effects in the aurora borealis and in the tails of comets and asteroids and meteors. Every rainbow is unique, differing from the angle and point of view of the specific observer. Every rainbow is temporary, always fleeting.

Rainbows kind of signify hope as well, and a bright side, a silver lining, a colorful light at the end of the darkened tunnel. There is always good despite the bad. I believe in that. I choose to believe in that. It might storm, it might sprinkle, it might be pouring out, but when that sun does come up in due time, the most beautiful and pure spectrum will stretch out across the vastness of sky. It is almost a reminder of the existential nature of our very lives. Rainbows are everywhere, every day, and everybody can see them if they just look hard enough, in the right places. Wake up. Take a step forward. Keep your eyes open. Chase after it. Search deep down inside of yourself. Go and find that rainbow . . .

ACKNOWLEDGEMENTS

First of all, I would like to thank my wife, Donna, for her ongoing encouragement and support. She has been such a blessing taking the lead on maintaining our household and caring for our one-year-old son, Andrew Nolan Gebhardt. It would not be possible to pursue this life path without her help. From waking up early every morning to maximizing every moment of free time to overcoming all of the challenges and setbacks, she has been my pillar and my muse. She was also a beta reader for four of the stories. Thank you, babe. We did it again.

Second, I want to thank my little brother, Daniel, who was the very first to believe in me and in my talents. Years ago, back when we both were living at home, I came out of our room with a binder full of secret work. I still remember him laughing out loud, enjoying it, impressed. I also still remember the typo he caught too. That was the initial step in following my dream and my passion. He was a beta reader for three of the stories. Also, my brother started a YouTube channel which I am frequently featured, PandaRoyale. Go and check us out.

I want to thank my writing partner, Jeremiah, who writes under JM Payer. We have been working together for many years ever since we met at NaNoWriMo. He was in the middle of transitioning between jobs, driving and flying back and forth, moving from different parts of the country, doing showings of his house, all while giving me much needed feedback on the manuscript. He helped thoroughly shape each of the five stories, the whole collection. His ripping apart my syntax and questioning my stylistic quirks raised the caliber of the prose. I am the writer I am today, thanks to his mentorship and his friendship.

I want to thank my first beta reader, Stephanie Takenaka. She provided extensive input on the earlier grammar and punctuation, and really pushed me towards publishing despite my many doubts at the time. She did beta reading for two of the stories. She also provided feedback on some of the language choices and on sensitivity issues.

My professional editor, Jennifer Fink, with her ten years of experience in academic, business and fiction editing as well as her background in language and literature helped give the final range of sight needed to wrap up this collection. Her punctuality, speed and expertise were a godsend. She did a wonderful job catching mistakes that went undetected.

I want to thank my proofreader, Mary Ervin. Her sincerity, responsiveness, work ethic, and thorough attention to detail were invaluable. From the copyright page to the afterword, she went through every single thing. More than that, she has been a great friend and source of positivity. This is the first work of mine she has been involved with.

I would also like to thank Tate Tsukamoto, the first writer friend I opened up to and who gave me input. To this day, him comparing one of my early pieces to something in Bamboo Ridge is still the best compliment ever. He did beta reading for two of the stories. He also provided feedback on language choices and sensitivity issues as well.

The professional team under Damon Freeman with their talent and experience working with some established and renowned authors brought this project together, turning this uncertainty into an absolute. Robynne was again a treasure, and I appreciate her patience and many accommodations. Karis did a wonderful job of molding my seemingly random ideas and vision into the perfect cover. Benjamin once again worked on the immaculate interior, all of the formatting and typesetting, and I'm grateful for his hard work.

Visit my website for more information about myself and about my writing. There are regular news announcements and a blog.

www.tjgiii.com

If you enjoyed this work, please leave a review on Amazon and on Goodreads. Every little bit counts and will help the collection get ranked in the algorithm for others to discover.

To stay up to date with all of the latest posts, follow me on social media. Every like, comment and follow is much appreciated.

www.facebook.com/tjg3words
www.instagram.com/tjg3words
www.twitter.com/tjg3words

This is the second book in an expanded literary universe. Here is a complete list of the other works available now.

Washington

ABOUT THE AUTHOR

Thomas J. Gebhardt III has been seriously writing for eight years after long days in healthcare, doing occupational therapy with the elderly. He lives with his wife and son in his hometown of Honolulu, Hawaii. He published his debut novel earlier this year, an anti-school shooting novel, and has talked with educators, survivors and concerned citizens, as well as donated to various charities. His work is heavily influenced by pop culture including movies, music, shows, video games, comic books, anime and manga.

www.ingramcontent.com/pod-product-compliance
Lightning Source LLC
Chambersburg PA
CBHW020140310726
48970CB00006B/1955